SAVED BY A LADY

Stringer gave a mighty heave and threw Cord over on his back. Then Stringer was atop him, and both his hands were around Cord's throat.

Cord tried to cock the revolver and his thumb slipped off the scored surface of the hammer. He dug in, got the hammer pulled back, fired again. The report was muffled by Stringer's flesh.

Stringer screamed and squeezed harder. Cord felt the hard muscle of his windpipe collapsing. He fired again, worked the hammer, pulled the trigger a fourth time.

The gun clicked empty.

Cord let it go, pried at Stringer's fingers. It was like trying to open a bear trap. Stars burst before Cord's eyes, burst and went out.

Through the enshrouding blackness he saw Chi somewhere up above him, her hands high over her head and in them a rifle barrel....

CORD

Brimstone Basin

Owen Rountree

BALLANTINE BOOKS • NEW YORK

Library of Congress Catalog Card Number: 86-90940

ISBN 0-345-32042-5

Manufactured in the United States of America

First Edition: November 1986

Chapter One

NATURE AWARDED SOME DAYS AS PREMIUMS, Cord thought: fine springtime days generally, when the clean look of fresh country was all your world; days of that sort, passed in open wilderness, were not debited against the sum of your mortal time. There was a notion: Chase territory and live forever.

This had been one of those days, and Cord had spent it riding the stage road that bisected the grassland country of central Montana. The road connected the railhead at Custer on the Yellowstone with the steamboat port at Fort Benton on the Missouri, according to the map on the wall of the Windmill Bar in Livingston. The map was tacked above the cashbox, and Cord studied it over the popping bubbles of a mug of lager beer. He was feeling impatient anyway, so the map was enough to get him restless. He wondered how that open range country lay, and who would travel it. The answers turned out to be pretty grand—and hardly anyone.

He'd seen his last itinerant ten miles back, a jug-eared boy afoot and leading a goat on a nubbly rope. The boy said, "Howdy" to Cord's greeting and "Over yonder" to Cord's question, pointing across the grass to the squat outline of a lopsided soddy. "Ma's a widder woman," the boy volunteered cheerlessly. "I am what she has got." When Cord gave him a silver dollar, the boy frowned and showed long brown teeth with a gap between the two in front. For some reason Cord felt embarrassed. "Well," he said. "So long." The boy frowned at the coin and did not look up.

Now, a couple hours later as the late spring sunset faded to barely color the crests of the mountains off west and cool night came on, Cord came up through the cut that the map in the Windmill Bar called South Gap. The moon, a few days shy of full, hung from cloudless sky to cast the faint outlines of dim shadows. By the road's side a milepost, repainted not too long before, announced that a town called Enterprise was seven miles ahead. Maybe an hour's ride, Cord reckoned. Enterprise would be the place to pass this night.

South Gap was a long shallow saucer in foothills cut with gully-washed breaks, most of the rivulets down to a muddy trickle as the season came toward summer. Cord pulled his bay gelding up to survey the lay of the prairie, the vast land washed white in the moonlight. The roll of the Little Belt Mountains stretched off to his left, the craggier frosted peaks of the Big Snowy Mountains to his right, the two ranges curving like open arms to encircle the great bowl of range called Bliss Basin.

Somebody had given it a good name. To Cord's mind, in which country was lately an ongoing concern, this territory in the spring season was all anybody could want, open and green and fertile. Cord squinted to see it as it had looked to the first whites to ride this sod and thought it was not so different. The buffalo were gone, but the elk would still string down to water, and deer would graze the free grass in herds of several dozen. Yet Cord envied those first lonesome men. They got to see the fresh thing.

Cord scraped a kitchen match over his thumbnail and examined his new gold pocket watch: It was coming up to nine-thirty. The watch snapped shut with satisfying precision. It was the best you could find in this end of the world, a present from his partner, Chi. She'd bought it for him out of poker winnings a few weeks back, the second watch she'd given him over the years. The first had been shattered in some old fracas. Cord could picture the broken watch staring up at him but forgot the exact circumstance and wondered if such forgetting was a sign of too much easiness in his life. He replaced the watch carefully in his vest pocket, handling it as if the case were eggshell. He suspected he was one of those people not meant to own a watch but hoped that with deliberation he could beat that particular aspect of his fate.

Nine-thirty and he was miles from bed. In the old days that would have meant nothing, but now he'd just as soon sleep between sheets and under a roof, all things being equal. He thumped the gelding and descended the sloping road toward the basin floor.

A ways ahead, thick lashings of willow below towering cottonwood marked the winding line of a meandering creek. The stage road dropped in parallel to it within another mile or so, and pretty soon the brush hemmed around and canopied the dirt track. Cord had meant to be off the trail by dark, and now that it had come on, he wished he'd been a tad more rigorous in his planning. The gelding shied back when Cord nudged him into the first reach of deep shadow, and Cord didn't blame him. Someone else was there.

The story had been vague and likely exaggerated, and the teller was an old greasy rider who looked to be heading for line camp, leading a packhorse loaded with a summer's grub. The old man wanted to talk, storing up conversation against the next couple months of high-country isolation, so Cord smoked a cigarette with him. The story had to do with stock rustling and vigilantism in Bliss Basin.

Mobs were in that category of dark uncontrollable threats that Cord feared, and now, in the shadows and tickled by that fear, Cord felt angry. He was no outlaw these days, and this darkening road was a public artery. Any money in his pocket was fairly earned and no one else's. There would be a public house in this Enterprise town, Cord decided; a town with a name like that ought to have amenities. He would have a drink of bourbon and a bed with linen in a room with a fireplace.

Cord urged the horse into the tunnel of brush. He'd take dinner as well: he fancied pork chops, with the fat browned and curling at the edges, and that morning's fresh bread with spring-cooled butter. Some dour Irishman's red-haired daughter checked into Cord's fantasy, serving up the meal on china plates chased with delicate blue veins. The girl had pale skin and a wise smile, and Cord was letting his mind drift toward naughty ideas and liking it when the gelding jerked up his head and spooked sideways.

Somewhere ahead horses were milling. Cord eased the gelding into the deeper shadow of the roadside and listened hard. An animal snorted wheezily and hooves tamped hard-packed dirt. More than a couple of men were talking in low hard voices.

Here was no business of his, Cord thought, no business and no trouble. He'd come on a string of roundup cowhands heading back to the wagon after some afternoon time in that town of Enterprise. They were likely getting ready to fort up in the abandoned soddy of some long-gone wolfer or road rancher.

Up ahead one of the riders laughed the kind of laugh that had more to do with another's distress than with humor. No trouble, Cord thought again, at least none having to do with him. The problem was, though, they were between him and his pork chops. Cord stayed where he was and felt a fool.

Plenty of guns went off all at once, crackling rifles and deeper booming handguns. The muzzle flashes were angry red firefly lights up the trail. The gelding stepped backward and Cord jerked at its head with his left hand. His Colt had gotten into his right.

Up there, a voice rich and thick as tapioca shouted, "Cease fire!" But the volley of gunfire had already ended a few moments earlier, as concertedly as it had begun. The stentorian voice called, "Sir—come out and face your judgment."

Cord sat his horse with the Colt in his hand. The moonlight silhouetted the limbs of the cottonwood crisscrossed above him, but thick darkness showed down the length of the tunnel of branches. The thing to do here, looking at it judiciously, was turn back, make a cold camp somewhere, and pass on whatever else this night was selling. Trouble was, if he rolled out his blankets on the ground, he'd be so pissed off at the faceless bastards who buffaloed him that he wouldn't sleep anyway. Just thinking about it now was getting him worked up. He was tired and going on up that road, and trouble belonged to the man who tried to stop him.

Cord holstered the Colt and drew his Winchester from its boot and held it ready across the fork of his saddle as he eased the gelding on up the road. Now he made out flickering flame, three or four small blazes, not a campfire but torches, moving and bobbing about. Cord climbed down off the gelding, looped the bridle reins around a clump of brush, and soft-footed along the roadside, an arm crooked up to keep branches from slapping him in the face. About fifty yards on, the road opened into a clearing, and there a wondrously odd and frightening sight confronted him.

Cord stared at the mounted band, and a quick chill washed through his marrow. He knew they were men but did not know what sort and so thought of headless specters and was frightened despite himself. After a moment, though, he made out what he was looking at. Instead of a hat, each man wore a hood of loosely draped black cloth, fastened around the forehead with a leather thong and cut with eye-holes. Each was draped in a long gray duster, like some Jayhawker. There were near to a dozen, some horseback, a couple afoot. Four carried flaming pitch-knot firebrands.

Then Cord saw that one man was hoodless and sat distinct from the others. Heavy-boned and stocky, he rode a tall wide palomino horse. His shoulders were broad and his features thick-ridged, and dense dark hair flowed over his shoulders in wavy tangles. A wide black leather belt was cinched over the blue-serge-and-brass-button uniform jacket of a Union captain. A holster depended from one side of the belt, home to a Colt single-action New Army revolver, and opposite hung an officer's scabbard. The big man held a long heavy saber aloft, where the torchlight drew flashing reflection from its wide blade.

Cord crouched on one knee at the edge of the clearing, holding the rifle and wondering what he figured to do with it. Across the opening, beyond a hard-packed dirt yard, was a plank-and-sod cabin set by a little gravel-bar rill in the creek. This was a rough and temporary sort of camp, without sign of husbandry or accommodation—no kitchen garden, chickens, wellhead, or washline, only a rude post-and-pole corral close by the cabin, in one of its corners a crude little shed open on two sides, a storage shelter for a few sacks of grain or a wagonload of hay. Six haltered horses ran loose in the corral.

"Damn you!" the big man shouted, a tremolo rippling along the base of his huge voice. Black powder smoke drifted in the night, and the rough-plank door of the soddy was splintered in the middle and half ripped from its leather hinges by the volley of gunfire. "May God damn you for a thief!"

Two of the hooded men stood before the crippled door, roughly gripping either arm of a third man. This one had the short neat figure of a jockey; he was a tight little fellow carrying no extra flesh at all. This man wore a baggy yellowish union suit. His feet were bare, his dirty hair bushy and uncombed, and the week's worth of whiskery stubble decorating his cheeks was shot with gray.

"Looks like you're fixing to do the job for Him," the little man said calmly.

Cord cast back into the past and came up with a name: Wilmer Blewin, known as Wee Bill. Cord was unsurprised to recognize the little man: The outlaw world was like a village, populated by no more than a few hundred people, and when you had lived in it as long as Cord had, you came to know your fellow townsfolk. Blewin was more of a visitor than a permanent resident, a now-and-again burglar and once-in-a-while robber who filled out his time with some legitimate work, mostly having to do with the stock-growing industry.

Then Cord remembered another man, Wee Bill's old partner, and scowled in the darkness, remembering as well some old personal trouble. Cord forgot the partner's name, or perhaps chose not to recollect. By then the man with the saber was shouting out another curse, and Cord came back: There was plenty enough trouble here and now.

Cord had never heard of Wee Bill doing any man killing, nor any other hanging crime. But here in this place, Cord smelled hanging's imminence.

The daft-looking old soldier with the saber jabbed his weapon at Wee Bill. He roared again, roared like a bear might, for the satisfaction of making the noise. It seemed to calm him for a moment, and he lowered the saber.

"Examine those horses," he growled, staring malediction at Wee Bill Blewin.

Here were the greasy cowhand's phantom night riders, in the flesh and ready for lynching. Cord stood there in the shadows tasting the rankness of foolish violence.

A man got down and shoved through the narrow gate into the corral, stepping in among the horses. "They're branded," he announced. "Every damned one of them." He ran his hand over a flank. "Some kind of Circle C, looks like."

"Does anyone know it?"

"Doesn't matter." Another man rode forward. "We know what we're about."

Could be Wee Bill had been doing some horse stealing somewhere, but Cord was not much taken with the idea of instant justice, especially in the hands of these mobsters. He knew he could not just go on crouching there in the night chill with his legs cramping up, waiting for the hand of God to intercede, and searched for ideas. He was shifting his weight when someone touched his back with a rifle barrel.

Cord froze, but the barrel jabbed painfully into his kidney anyway. "Been watching you since you stopped on the road, looking this way and that, deciding." Cord felt breath on the back of his neck. "You made a bad choice."

Cord put his rifle on the ground and raised his hands. The Winchester snaked back and away. "Now we stand up," the man behind him said. When he did, Cord caught a glimpse of the man's black hood. A moment later, Cord's Colt ceased to make weight on his right hip.

Another hooded man rode up the track leading Cord's horse and another. The man behind Cord tossed the Winchester up to his buddy, who leaned back and slipped it into its scabbard.

"Captain Bliss!" The man jabbed Cord again, pushing him toward the clearing.

The big man with the saber turned and frowned in the light of the burning flares.

"Take it easy with that goddamn rifle," Cord said.

This bought him a little snap of a pistol barrel against the back of his head, a sharp hard knock designed for pain but not to put him down. "How's that again?" The man behind him sneered.

Captain Bliss watched them come into the clearing. Wee Bill Blewin grinned at Cord, nooded, and said, "I'll be dipped."

"Your partner returns," Bliss announced with satisfaction.

"He ain't no pard of mine," Wee Bill said neutrally.

"An acquaintance, perhaps," Bliss said. "A colleague."

This was starting to move in dangerous directions, Cord thought. Bliss stared at him. "I know you," he said.

"No, you don't."

"My man," Bliss said. "As there is no duly sanctioned law in this basin, it falls to those who claim the country as their own to promote order. I do what I must for peace."

"You got odd ideas about what constitutes peace," Cord said.

"Rustling finds no haven here." Bliss peered down at him. "Nor does outlawry." He smiled with satisfaction. "I have arranged with the territorial attorney in Helena to send all Wanted posters to my attention. Your face has graced several, Mister Cord."

"There's a break for us." The right sleeve of one man's duster was empty and pinned up at the shoulder. "Once we hang him, we can sleep easy, knowing we done the law a good turn."

"Those posters are from another time," Cord said. "I'm not wanted for a damned thing."

"What are you doing here?"

"Getting annoyed," Cord snapped. "You give some thought to what you are about. They hang murderers in this territory. There is law—"

"I am the law," Bliss barked. "I read its letter and invoke its spirit. I rule in this basin."

"Sure enough," the man behind Cord said. "His Highness the Emperor Bliss."

"Shut up," Bliss ordered. He shook his head. "Do nothing, sir," he said to Cord. "We will see to you after our primary business." Bliss aimed the saber at Wee Bill Blewin. "You, sir, are a rustler."

"Says you," Wee Bill answered with fair calmness. He was showing some sand, dragged out in the night and facing death in his underwear. He was slow to surrender his dignity; in this coolness Cord read innocence.

"Do you claim to own these horses?" Bliss demanded. "I will see your proof."

Wee Bill spat in the dirt. "That so?" He glanced over at Cord and winked. Cord drew quick breath against the gun barrel hard in his back.

"You rustled them."

"No," Wee Bill said, looking Bliss right in the eye.

Bliss returned a look hard as blade steel.

"You are determined to murder me dead," Wee Bill said. "Nothing I can say nor do will change that."

"You got that part reckoned right." The speaker, astride a black horse, was disguised as the others in the night rider's uniform of hood and duster, but he stood out for his size: his bulky mass was nearly a match for Bliss's. He rode a horse big enough for him, with three white-stockinged feet. Cord noted his boots—he'd seen the like before: of heavy stiffened black leather, with big brass buckles on the saddle straps and blocked-off toes that were likely lined with sheet steel. These were fighting boots, designed to give the wearer the edge soon as the brawling started, and to inflict maximum bone-breaking damage as it progressed.

Bliss leaned in the saddle and said something in a low deep voice to the man in the fighting boots. The man laughed. Bliss jerked angrily away from him, shook his head. The other man laughed again and twisted around in the saddle to look over Cord. Behind the hood's peepholes, the man's eyes sparkled in the torchlight; he looked like something carved for Halloween, and Cord thought of the Headless Horseman in the boys' tale.

The man at Cord's back said, "Guess how you end up?"

Cord started. He had not thought it through that far, had

not credited the perverse notion that a nighttime ride could lead to the end of a rope. But they figured him for Wee Bill's partner—or not, maybe only a passing rider who'd already seen too much to be left alive. . . . it came to the same thing. The darkness of real anger began to fall over Cord's eyes. *Jesus Christ—it was too pointless: hung dead for bad timing. . . .*

"Hey now," Cord said.

Bliss pulled his horse back, stared down at Cord. "Bind him," Bliss said.

The rifle barrel stayed hard into Cord's back while someone tied his wrists with a bit of rope, jerking the knots tight. Cord's eyes watered.

"I told you to be still, sir." But a faint tinge of regret had crept into Bliss's tone.

Cord's captor said, "Let's go take in the show," in Cord's right ear. The gun came away from Cord's back, but then the man jerked up hard on his bound wrists, pushing Cord forward and levering pain from his shoulder joints.

Bliss had forgotten him. He stared down at Wee Bill Blewin from a great calm distance. "Now sir, is the time to speak in your defense."

Wee Bill worried at his lower lip with his teeth, as if considering how to tell it. "Them horses . . ."

"Yes?"

"You hear of Albert Canaday?" Wee Bill asked. "Runs maybe eight hundred head of cows and horses near Buffalo, Wyoming?"

"No sir," Bliss rumbled. His voice, when calm, sounded like a storm beyond a far mountain range.

"This Canaday has sold them horses to a Rocky Boy Indian, name of Petey Greentree, up on Milk River. Me and my partner is hired to trail them up there."

Bliss cocked his head toward Cord and kept his eye on Wee Bill. "This man," he declared.

Wee Bill looked around. "Anyone got a smoke?" he asked.

"Where is your partner?" Bliss demanded.

"Went into town."

"What the hell?" the man in the square-toed boots growled. "We come here to do business or to powwow?"

Bliss said to Wee Bill, "You can produce a bill of sale?"

For the first time, uncertainty colored the little man's features. "My partner's got it."

Bliss's bushy dark eyebrows furrowed in a deep V, but the rest of the men burst into laughter. Wee Bill smiled as if in on the joke. "You do mean to string me," he said softly.

"Save yourself."

Wee Bill snorted.

"Name your partner—if he exists."

Wee Bill seemed to consider the offer. "I guess I won't," he said.

"We shall do what we came for," Bliss announced.

"I figured," Wee Bill said, almost amiably, "starting about when you blew my door in and rousted me out of bed." He looked around at the hooded men. "Wish there'd been a little more warning, give me time to pull on my britches at least."

"Proceed," Bliss called out.

"Anyway," Wee Bill said, "soon as it begun, I could see clear through to the end." He reflected. "Though I will say that knowing how it comes out don't make it easier to live through."

But Bliss had backed his horse away, and no one was listening to Wee Bill now except for Cord.

"You and you." The man in the fighting boots picked

out two men. "See if there is anything we can use in that cabin." He looked around at the others. "You-all know what to do."

The night riders moved with concert and precision now, as if they had drilled at the payoff to this drama or played it out enough before to have it down pat. Two men rode around to the side of the corral, bent in the saddle, and worked one of the fence rails loose from either end. Raising it over their heads, they propped it across the six-foot space between the cabin's flat roof and the top of the wall of the open-sided feed shed. It formed a crossbeam maybe eight feet above the dirt yard.

Two men came out of the cabin: one carried a lantern, the other a tin can of coal oil.

"No!" Bliss said. "Do you wish to burn down this basin?"

"Just this rustlers' roost," the man in the fighting boots said. "Look around." The soddy was surrounded by bare yard on every side. "This ain't grass-fire weather anyway," he went on. Before Bliss could object further, he barked orders: "Couple of you get them horses out and down the road apiece. We don't want them spooking on us."

A hangman's noose had already been fashioned in the thick hemp rope that another man flung over the rail. He took several turns of the loose end around his saddle horn, backed his horse so the loop hung about head-level off the ground. Across the corral, mounted men got the last of the horses out and moved them down the dirt track, careful to keep them well away from the torch fire.

The men flanking Wee Bill had his little wrists tied up tight and were hustling him over beneath the beam. No one made jokes now or spoke at all as a man settled the rope over Wee Bill's head and around his neck, jerked ragged stray strands of his hair out of the way, slipped the knot up tight under his right ear. The night riders had come to see the life choked out of a man while he hung kicking like a frog, and now it was about to happen. The hangman backed his horse another step to make the rope taut and pulled Wee Bill erect but not quite off the ground. The mob watched in awed silence, fascinated at the fragility of life and their power to stop it cold, easy as smashing a watch with a hammer. Faces shined brightly in the irregular light, impassioned at the forbidden sight of death, and relieved: It was not them. The little man's mortality was not theirs, so from his death they drew some dark, half-formed, perverse reassurance of life. They were of that sort.

Cord felt sick.

Wee Bill rose on his toes to take the pressure off the rope.

"Wait one minute." Cord's voice sounded tight, as if the rope girded his own throat. He spoke louder. "One goddamned minute."

Someone snickered, and someone else said, "Getting ready to piss his pants," but for the moment they were watching him. Bliss frowned with distaste, raised his saber high over his head. "Prepare to carry out justice," he ordered, and the moment was broken.

"You are in one hell of a hurry to murder," Cord said desperately. The man with the kerosene began splashing it over the wood facade of the soddy, tossed what was left onto the shed.

"Lock him up," Cord pressed. "Check his story, find this Canaday . . ."

"There is no Canaday." Bliss's fervor was rising, and Cord felt that at this moment all of this business tottered on an edge, below which lay abyss. "There is no bill of sale. There is only this rustler, his crime and his condemnation, and God's mercy on his soul."

But Wee Bill had awakened to this last slim chance of salvation. "What he said." He jutted his chin in Cord's direction. "There are ways you could learn if I am smoking you."

"We came for hanging," the man in the fighting boots insisted.

"Listen." Now, finally, Wee Bill was pleading.

"Do him." There was threat and command in the voice of the man in the fighting boots, and Bliss heard it and the message it conveyed: He could exercise his authority or have it seized. Bliss stared back from under his thick eyebrows and brought the saber down in a broad sweep.

The hangman jerked hard on his reins and his horse raised up its head, snorted, and abruptly backed away several surprised steps. Wee Bill was jerked off the ground so quickly and violently his head banged against the beam. The hangman held his horse and Wee Bill's weight fell against the rope's tension. That did it: his neck snapped, and he was hanged.

The hangman walked his horse forward, and Wee Bill's corpse collapsed liquidly to the dirt. A rich stink rose from him. Someone worked the rope from his neck. A bit of blood flowed between Wee Bill's lips. Another night rider was crouched beside him; when he rose and stepped away, Cord saw the placard pinned to the front of Wee Bill's union suit: HORSE THIEF.

"Fire 'em up?" One of the torchmen looked around and blinked, the first violation of the silence that had descended on the clearing.

"Not just yet." It was the man in the fighting boots, and

he was looking at Cord. Bliss stared fervently at the body and did not seem to hear.

"Your turn," the man behind Cord said, and pushed him forward.

Bliss jerked his head up. There was possession and ardor in his dark coarse face, and something that could have been madness. "Now then sir," he said, and closed his mouth, as if he had lost the thread.

"Forget that shit," the man in fighting boots said. "We got to string him, whatever."

"Is that so?" Bliss said dangerously.

Cord listened to them talk about murdering him and tried to marshal his thoughts into a search party for solutions. He had faced plenty enough deadly situations and walked away whole, mostly because he kept his head and did not give up, partly because he'd had some luck. But right now no plan came to mind because none existed, and luck had gone south at the last fork.

"Listen close, old man," the man in the fighting boots said. "Figure out whose balls get squeezed if we let this hombre live. Whose name does he know, whose name and whose face?" He laughed. "How do you like it, Captain Mallory Bliss?"

"You cur," Bliss said.

"Sure," the other man said amiably.

Cord heard agreement in the murmurs of the other men. "We already hung four of these bastards this week," one said. "Another ain't gonna hurt."

"We finish up," the man with the lantern said, "then get outside a drink of whiskey."

One good idea, Cord thought desperately. There was a path out of this madness, and all he need do was discover one good idea for finding it. Hands prodded at him and walked him forward and got the coarse stiff rope over his ears. As it passed before his eyes, Cord thought he saw where one turn of the hemp was wet and dark with Wee Bill's blood. It settled around his neck, the knot tight against his jugular.

Cord saw Bliss, staring back at him up there horseback, his dark eyes blank and bottomless. To one side, a man whirled the lantern around his head, whooped, and flung it into the soddy door. The lamp disintegrated in an explosion of glass and a splash of liquid flame that washed the front of the cabin. A rider threw his torch into the old dry hay on the floor of the shed. Fire climbed its wall.

The hangman stepped his horse back. Cord tensed the muscles in his neck, tried to make them hard as iron against the crushing pressure. Strands of the rope prickled his flesh like needles. Above him, the fires had reached either end of the beam over which the rope was dangling. The insistent pull lifted Cord's bootheels from the hard-packed dirt. He stumbled, and the rope held him upright and dug into the softness beneath his chin.

A horse squealed at the fire and pawed the ground, kicking up gravel. Cord felt bits of it against his pants leg. The hangman pulled his horse back and Cord stood on toe tips, twisting at the rope's end. The fire enveloped the walls to either side, seared at him, toasting his skin red. Above, flames walked along the beam to a meeting where the rope hung. The hangman laughed, and the rope jerked sharply.

Cord's windpipe closed up, and he was lifted part of the way clear of the ground, and then he was hanging free and could not breathe at all. He swung in the air and heard the fire crackling and men calling out and horses blowing, all against the roar of blood pounding and rushing in his ears.

The blood had colored his vision as well, or perhaps it

was the fire, but when Cord glimpsed Bliss, it was through a crimson veil. Involuntarily, Cord swung backward at the rope's end. Bliss jerked away from another man, slashed wildly with the saber at Cord. The blade swept past Cord's eyes, flashing blood-red in the firelight, and came around again backhand to meet Cord's body as he swung forward.

Someone cursed. The blade passed over Cord's head and the rope jerked hard. He saw men struggling above him, saw the saber's blade cross his field of vision another time; the rope twanged once more and let him down. Cord fell, crumpled hard to the ground; loose rope puddled atop him.

Still he could not breathe; the noose was vise-tight around his windpipe, and he could not draw air past it or get his hands out from behind to loosen the rope's coil. Sweat burned his eyes. It was like drowning in lava. . . .

Above Cord, the fire-weakened beam crackled and tore. He looked through the sweat, and fire was raining down in his face. He tried to roll free but could move hardly at all, so the flames came down all around him and very close, enveloping him in their scorching heat. He felt burning pain but dimly, dully because numbness was taking over, starting at his closed throat and racing everywhere through his body.

Cord closed his eyes. For just a moment he saw red fire still, but then it winked out and was replaced by a long tunnel of cool blackness. Cord lunged forward and escaped into it.

Chapter Two

"**O**NCE UPON A TIME," CHI SAID, "THERE WAS a *bandido*. This was years ago, in another country."

The man across from her smiled vaguely and leaned back in his chair to cross his legs.

"A robber," Chi said. "Banks, trains, stagecoachs. His name was Rogelio Duro, but I am going to call him Hardiman."

"Why?" the man asked.

"Because this is my story," Chi said. "And I can tell it any goddamned way I please." But she didn't sound angry.

"Yes you can," the man said. He was clean-shaven and had regular handsome features and very white teeth.

"Greed and sloth," Chi said.

The man looked at her narrowly.

"The reasons most folk turn to banditry." Chi frowned. "What is your name?"

"Stern," the man said. "I already told you, twice."

"I forgot," Chi said. "Both times." Late afternoon sun streaked through the greasy window above the table. Oasis Saloon was stenciled on it in an arch of four-inch letters that framed the railroad station across the street; the shingle hanging from the rain gutter over the station's short end marked this stop as Big Timber. "But not Hardiman," Chi said.

Stern looked confused. "What about Hardiman?"

"Hardiman turned to banditry for love," Chi said.

"I should have guessed," Stern said, and waved his left hand. He had card player's fingers, long and thin with clean, shapely nails.

"He was young, and there was a woman. She was older than he, handsome and dark."

"Like you," Stern said.

Chi shook her head. "Not me." She flashed a quick brittle smile. "I don't like *chiquitos*."

But actually this Stern was not so much younger than she; somewhere around thirty, Chi guessed. He wore black gabardine trousers and a matching vest; a new brown felt hat with a narrow flat brim and a flat crown lay upright on the table to his right. He had nice hair, blond and wavy, and every now and then he smoothed the sides of it with the palms of his hands. She could stand that, but she didn't like his ruffled white shirt.

"This Hardiman," Chi said. "He thought the woman would like him more if he had plenty of money."

"That works sometimes," Stern said carefully.

Chi shrugged. "Money never hurts." The tequila bottle at her right elbow was two-thirds empty; the first sip from it had been breakfast. "Hardiman determined to steal enough to please her," Chi said. "If he died trying, he imagined she would mourn him, which was another way to have her heart."

"Second best choice, though," Stern said.

"You find this too romantic to believe?"

Stern shrugged.

Chi held the bottle by the neck. The Oasis Saloon was pleasant enough for day drinking. There was a brass rail along the foot of the bar and sawdust on the floor, scattered around a fat cast-iron stove. Its firebox was cold, for this was a fine spring day. The bartender had a fringe of white hair like a tonsure and shiny fat white cheeks and cheerful pink eyes.

Customers came and went. If any were bemused or titillated or annoyed by the presence of a handsome tequila-drinking brown woman, they had the manners or good sense to keep it to themselves. So no one had bothered her, except maybe Stern. He bothered her a little.

Chi filled the shot glass in front of her, pouring a thin ribbon of tequila into the exact center of the false bottom until the meniscus of the liquor bulged up above the rim. "Well, it's true," Chi said, as if Stern had gainsaid her.

Stern's fluted double-shot glass remained half-full of Kentucky sour mash table whiskey. Here was the sort of man who did not like liquor and never had but learned to drink it so he could be around without attracting attention. "Tell your tale," Stern said.

"Tiene prisa?" Chi snapped.

Stern shook his head no. "I got plenty of time."

Chi raised her shot glass in a rock-steady hand and drank down the tequila. "Your pard there, though, he's starting to get skittish." She cocked her head toward the bar and watched Stern.

The kid at the bar had almost no chin and wore trail

clothes. He was drinking beer, half facing away. Chi looked at him over her shoulder. The chinless kid swiveled away and put both elbows on the bar. There was an oil painting of a naked woman over the whiskey shelf, but he kept his eyes down.

Chi turned back to Stern. He had stopped smiling. He watched Chi take out a leather pouch, worry open the drawstring.

"I watched you play cards yesterday, in that other place." Chi fished out a brown leaf of cigarette paper. "And that rat-faced boy, wandering around the table, peeking and peering, tipping you to other people's hands."

"How was he doing that?" Stern asked neutrally.

"Every time it got down to you and one other player," Chi said, "your boy tried to get himself a look at the other fellow's hole cards. I remember him bending down to tuck in his pant leg a lot."

Stern put on a skeptical look.

"When it worked," Chi said, "he cued you if the other hombre had the tickets."

"How did he do that?"

"He lit up a smoke." Chi laughed. "That all you can think of for the signal? Don't you have any imagination?"

Stern turned the glass between his long, pretty hands. "Are you calling me a card cheat?"

"Oh yes," Chi said. "Yes indeed."

"Miss Chi," Stern said, courtly. "You are drunk."

She looked at him blankly. A moment passed during which she could have taken it as an insult or let it pass, when she could have gone into blind rage or raucous laughter. She didn't know herself for that moment which way she was heading, nor much care. This Stern had better watch his step. . . .

Stern had uncrossed his legs and looked a little like her expression bothered him. But then Chi laughed. "*Por supuesto*," she agreed amiably. She shook tobacco into a creased paper, twisted it up between her fingers, and pulled the drawstring tight.

Stern struck a match with his thumbnail and held it out.

Chi ignored it. She pointed at Stern with her cigarette, and her voice was hard and cold and nothing drunk in it at all. Right now she liked hearing herself this way. "I am drunk," Chi said, "and you are a sharper and a cheat, trying to court my favor. No telling what you want." She shook her head and contracted herself. "Yeah, there is, when I think about it. I guess we both know what you are after."

Stern gaped at her.

"Someone is looking for trouble," Chi said.

"Not me," Stern said.

"Me," Chi said. "I am."

The match burned down to Stern's fingers. He grimaced and waved it out, dropped the charred stick on the scarred tabletop.

Chi put the cigarette in her mouth. "You got a light?" she asked sweetly.

Stern stared at her half-shrewdly. He looked like a man thinking he might have taken a wrong turn and wondering if it would be shorter to go back or on ahead. He shook his head and pushed his chair away from the table, started to rise.

"Where you going?" Chi said. "Drink your drink."

Stern put charm in his smile, and said, "I won't intrude if I'm not sure I'm welcome."

Chi stabbed a finger across the table. "Drink your god-damned drink, *cabrón*."

Stern lowered his ass back into his seat. He picked up

the double-shot glass in three fingers and drank down the straight whiskey.

"You stick around," Chi said, "and maybe your dreams will come true after all."

A good deal of the light in Stern's smile had gone out. In what was left, Chi read his hope that there might be some shot at her after all. "Figuring odds?" she asked. "Looking at the size of the bet against the money in the pot?"

Stern said, "Why do you want to be this way?" honestly enough that she almost felt sorry for an instant. She turned away and called, "*Mesonero*."

The bartender came to the table with a sqaurish bottle of whiskey labeled Heaven's Kiss Sour Mash Whiskey. He said, "I like being called that. Finer than barkeep, and smoother on the ear." When he filled Stern's glass, his pink eyes flashed happily.

Chi produced a one-dollar note, and when the little bartender took it, she patted him on his shiny fat cheek. "Oh, my," the bartender said brightly. His cheek quivered like a big dog's jowls.

"Drink up," Chi said to Stern.

Stern studied the drink. "Maybe we ought to eat a bite," he said. "After that we can work out some plans for this fine evening."

Chi looked past him out the window and shook her head with something like sadness. "My right hand," she said.

"Yes?" Stern could not see where this was going.

"Guess what is pointed at you under this table. Guess what part it is aimed at."

"That's a poor joke."

From beneath the center of the table came the unique click of a revolver's hammer being cocked.

The last of Stern's smile quick-froze. His eyes looked rheumy.

"Having a woman like me," Chi said, "has got to be dangerous. Otherwise where is the fun in it?" She picked up her glass in her left hand and drank.

Chi rapped the underside of the table with her gun barrel, and Stern started. "Play along," Chi said. The hammer of her gun clicked down again, and in a moment her right hand appeared above the table.

"You are addled," Stern said.

"Doesn't matter," Chi said. "You still got to hear my story."

Stern's shoulders relaxed, and he ran both palms along the wavy sides of his blond hair. Chi folded her arms and leaned forward and pointed at the cigarette in her mouth; Stern hesitated a moment, then passed another match to her. She struck it on the underside of the thigh of her black britches. A woolen serape was draped over her shoulders, and her flat-brimmed black sombrero hung from a thong beneath her chin.

When she picked up the story again, she told it seriously enough, but at first Stern listened warily, as if he feared this was bait for some other demeaning trap. But Chi no longer smiled and seemed to choose her words with some care, pausing now and then as if to get them exactly right. Once she stopped to refill her shot glass and another time to crush out the butt of the thin brown cigarette under her high bootheel, but otherwise she went at it in a straight line from there on. Stern relaxed and smiled his thin smile now and then, as if he were still preoccupied with possibilities involving the two of them.

But presently, as the tale began to take shape, he was drawn in despite himself. He propped his elbows on the table and listened with genuine interest and little interruption.

The man Chi called Hardiman was a boy at the time in which her story began, perhaps seventeen years old and *muy simpático*. The woman was much older (Chi said), twenty-five or -six, experienced with the world and men, and she teased him and would not take him seriously. "He was sensitive," Chi said. "He wrote poems." He had a sensitive boy's ideas: He would end up rich and happy or dead and well-grieved. "Hardiman could not lose," Chi said.

"I'll bet he did, though," Stern said. "Otherwise where is the story?"

"Listen to what happened," Chi said.

No robber was ever as dumb or wrong-headed as this Hardiman boy, Chi went on. If he had a reason for picking the bank he chose, no one ever knew what it was.

It was a small establishment in a backland town that Chi called Victoria. On the way, Hardiman had a whiskey or three for his nerves and, thinking to do some business with his drinking, asked a bunch of questions about the Victoria Bank. A sheriff overheard all this and rode out ahead.

Hardiman hit Victoria about midday, and by then the sheriff had time to make a few arrangements. Two men with rifles were hunkered behind the false front on the roof of the mercantile across the dirt street from the bank, and the vault was locked up tight. The sheriff borrowed the cashier's green eyeshade and took his place, his pistol close to hand in a half-open cash drawer. The bank president could not be persuaded to leave, though; he stood his ground by the vault, as if the money were his.

Hardiman rode in, hitched his horse in front of the Victoria Bank, and looked around the noonday street. There was no mistaking him because he pulled his neckerchief over his face in proper outlaw style and took out his pistol, right there in the street. But the riflemen on the roof were too young to be veterans of the war and thus not hardened to the idea of gunning a man down in cold blood. While they hesitated, Hardiman went inside.

The sheriff saw the gun and kept his mouth shut, but the banker said something like "What is the meaning of this, young man?" The sheriff's hand crept into the cash drawer toward his gun, thinking out his play and careful not to push it, figuring time was on his side. Meanwhile Hardiman was ordering the banker to open the vault, and the banker was refusing. About then the street door opened, and several things happened quickly, one after another.

It had not occurred to Hardiman that anyone might interrupt his business, and he turned abruptly. A middle-aged capitalist was holding the bank door for a young bonneted woman carrying a tiny baby. Hardiman took a step toward them, tripped over his own boots, and stumbled into the cash drawer, slamming it on the sheriff's fingers. The sheriff yowled, the woman saw Hardiman's gun and screamed, and the baby began to bawl. The woman shut her mouth and fainted, but she held on to the baby. It bounced off her stomach and rolled onto the floor, unhurt but damned surprised.

Hardiman saw the capitalist reach inside his coat and, misreading the move, snapped, "Bring it out slow." The capitalist produced a bulging pocketbook. Hardiman did not know this was a wealthy feed-and-grain speculator or that the man had cleaned the table at the monthly poker game with his rich cronies, but he knew enough to grab the man's poke and stuff it in his shirt.

The baby was screaming, the sheriff was swearing with his mouth full of broken fingers, and the banker snorted with outrage. He went to his desk and rummaged in the top drawer, too single-minded to be frightened. Meanwhile the woman was coming around, to Hardiman's relief. Still, there was no telling what sort of voice she'd add to the din, so Hardiman shoved his gun in his holster and hit the road.

He realized his horse was gone about a second and a half before the two men on the rooftop across the way emptied their magazines in a wild spray of shots, none of which came too close. At about the same time, a big farm kid in coveralls and no shirt came lumbering down the street astride a big yellow Belgian draft animal with a rope hackamore and no saddle.

At the gunfire, the farm horse rolled its eyes, snorted, and thundered up on the boardwalk in front of the bank. The canopy clotheslined the big kid. He tumbled off into the dirt, made his feet with surprising speed, and skedaddled. Hardiman dragged the horse back down to the street and swung onto its back.

By then the marksmen had gotten reloaded, and they let go at Hardiman at about the same time the banker came running out the door firing a short-barreled revolver fast as he could cock the hammer and pull the trigger. Hardiman's gun was still in his holster; he seemed to have forgotten it was available.

The banker missed twice and then shot Hardiman in the gut, bending him over double. The farm horse stumbled, and Hardiman grunted and jerked hard on the rope bridle, but the panicked horse shied around the wrong way. The banker's fourth shot slammed right into Hardiman's chest. It hurt instantly and massively, and he was pretty sure he was dead. Before he could decide absolutely, another bullet struck his head and everything got dimmer.

Chi stopped at that point in the story to concentrate on

fashioning a cigarette. Stern watched her hands, not missing the fact that they were a tiny bit less steady. "Bank robbing is not my line," Stern said. "But I would rate it risky business in the best of circumstances. The way this boy went at it, he was asking to die."

"That's what I said," Chi said impatiently. "When I started this story."

"That's so," Stern admitted.

"Only he didn't."

"Didn't what?"

"Die," Chi said.

At seventeen you are tougher than you know, Chi told Stern, and Hardiman managed to hang on to the big Belgian and some bit of consciousness until he got to a fair-sized creek. He sent the horse running for home with a swat and waded upstream. He got about a half mile and into a thicket of willow before passing out for good. He did not come to until the next morning, so he never knew that mounted men passed him close by in the dark three times.

Hardiman lay still and kept his eyes closed for a bit; he hurt like hell and wasn't sure he wanted to know why. But then, with the sun climbing into the sky of a new day, Hardiman dragged himself up against a tree trunk and took inventory. The more he discovered, the more he marveled.

The last shot, the one that had caught him in the head, was the only one that had done anything that could really be called harm, and most of that was to his sombrero. A hole had been torn in the front and back of its felt crown, and when Hardiman took it off and touched at the top of his head, he found a sticky line running about where the part would have been if Hardiman had combed his hair to either side. Even then there was not so much blood, and no double vision or fuddle-mindedness, and the pain was not as bad as the previous night's blackout headache.

"You are ribbing me, right?" Stern said then. "You get this Hardiman shot in the tripes and the heart, and now you have him sitting up counting his blessings. Is this tree in the hereafter?"

Chi nodded happily, as if Stern had gotten it just right. "That is what Hardiman wondered, soon as he worried up a clear recollection of the day before and the other two slugs hitting him. He felt around his stomach and his chest, and now that he was paying attention he noticed his whole body ached like hell." Chi drank her glass of tequila and refilled it. There was an inch of the colorless liquor left in the bottle. "But," Chi said, "no blood."

Behind Chi, someone said, "You gonna be long." It was the rat-faced boy, Stern's cardsharping confederate.

"Go somewhere," Stern said. He smiled at Chi. "You are not needed here."

"No dumb card-flashing sheep wanted hereabouts," Chi confirmed nastily. Behind her, the boy drew a sharp breath. "Get," she said, returning Stern's smile, as if this were a lovers' game they both knew well.

The boy thought it over a moment too long. Chi spun around and came out of her chair. She kicked the boy hard in the shin, and when he yowled and jerked up one leg and hopped almost comically, she knocked him down. She did not punch him but merely pushed him over with both hands, which was meant to humiliate him and did. The boy fell over a chair and lay there looking up at her through hurt eyes.

For a moment she felt bad and wondered why she was acting like this. But she knew the answer to that, and not liking herself so much at this moment was one thing and suffering the presence of simpletons and mooncalves was another. She saw the sweet old bartender from the corner of her eye: he looked sad. "You get, boy," she said in a mean voice to the kid on the floor. She could do what she wanted, and everyone else could like it or stand the hell out of her way. The kid got to his feet and sidled out the door.

Stern didn't look too put out, considering he had called the boy partner, but there was a word that meant different things to different people. He was looking at her curiously and amused when she sat down, the way you might regard a pup while trying to decide whether to whip or pet it. But she was nobody's pup.

Chi put her smile back on and said again, "No blood."

Stern laughed and shook his head. "Imagine that."

"Pay attention." Chi waggled a finger under his nose, as if this was a fine flirt they shared. "Hardiman grabbed at his belt to undo his britches, and the leather parted in his hands. The buckle was a big square of solid silver worked with turquoise, and in its middle was a huge dimple where one fat slug had hit him. It had stretched and weakened the leather and hammered the buckle hard into his belly, but there was no hole—in the buckle or in him.

"Once he got over that," Chi said, "Hardiman ripped open the front of his union suit, and the fat pocketbook of currency fell out. Hardiman had forgotten about the money, but right then it was not what had his eye. The whole front of his stomach and chest was black-and-yellow and blue-and-purple, from his bellybutton up to his throat." Chi drank down her tequila and began to build another smoke. "And in the middle of his breastbone, right over where his heart would be, a bullet was sticking out of him."

"See here!"

"Hardiman slapped at it like it was a hornet, and the

bullet fell away. There was a little circle of ragged torn flesh under it, a *pendejo* or two deep, no more." Chi touched herself between her breasts. "The muscle is hardly a half inch thick right there, but this bullet stopped before it reached bone. A scratch."

Chi drank. "But the pocketbook full of money was drilled right through the middle."

Stern reached across the table for her bottle, meaning to refill her glass. Chi said, "Don't." Stern leaned back in his chair, too casually. "Is this a true story?" he asked.

"Why do you care?"

"I don't know." Stern sounded genuinely perplexed. "What are we talking about? What parts am I supposed to believe?"

Chi felt the anger coming back. She poured the last of the tequila into her glass, and what was left filled it right to the rim without a drop splashing over. She let it sit. This would be the last one. One quart of liquor was enough for today. She told the rest of it quickly and dispassionately, as if she might have given Stern too much credit for perception and companionability.

Hardiman looked at the holes drilled in his hat and buckle and stolen money and contemplated the entirety of his own body, and saw the hand of a higher power. What had happened was uncreditable except by faith. Hardiman decided he was chosen.

He forgot the woman and gave his love to fate, risk, and outlawry. Within six months he was notorious and within a year he was legendary. He wore the hat and buckle like emblems and gave away notes of punctured currency as his sign, his mark. He had plenty by then.

Other robbers flocked to him for his luck, only to learn that his magic did not extend to others. Men joined his bunch and died, while Hardiman remained always charmed. Hardiman was destiny's darling and he never feared.

Then, one day years later in a town not far from Victoria, Hardiman walked out of a bank with some of its money, and someone put a gun barrel against the side of his head.

When this had happened before, Hardiman knocked the gun away and disarmed whoever was foolish enough to challenge his enchantment. This time he hesitated for some reason. It occurred to him later that he may have recognized the voice or manner or something about the man who ordered his hands up. In the end, though, he decided his hesitation was preordained, as much a product of fate as his gift.

The man came around to where Hardiman could see him: it was the sheriff from the bank in Victoria all those years ago, gray and balding now. He no longer wore a badge; his sheriffing days were behind him. His revolver looked about as ancient as he, a skinny old Colt Navy .38 with rust on the frame and barrel. But the tip of the cartridge in the cylinder looked huge and past them Hardiman saw dangerous emotion on the old man's face.

It frightened him.

"Come around," the ex-sheriff said, and led him behind the building, poking at him with the gun.

The one-time law dog was an addled old jasper now, and Hardiman had laughed in the face of men ten times as dangerous. But right then the chance of Hardiman disarming the old man was about on a par with levitation. Fear tasted bitter in Hardiman's mouth and sat heavy on his gut. It mystified and stupefied him.

Behind the bank in a barren vacant lot, the ex-sheriff turned Hardiman around and stepped back a yard or two, keeping the gun carefully lined on Hardiman's face. "Lookee here," the ex-sheriff said, and at first Hardiman thought that was the signal for shooting. The fear was nauseating him; if he could move he would vomit.

Sweat blurred his vision, so at first he made out only a shape waving back and forth. Hardiman blinked. The ex-sheriff was holding the rust-flecked revolver in his left hand and showing Hardiman his right. "Look here," the ex-sheriff insisted. Three of his fingers were stiff and useless and pointed in odd directions, and Hardiman remembered the gun in the cash drawer. "How charmed are you feeling now, you finger-busting son of a bitch?"

Hardiman thought his knees would buckle, but before that could happen, the ex-sheriff took a step back and gasped and pulled the trigger.

The gun went off with a tremendous roar, and something seared into Hardiman's cheek. It pained him but did not knock him down. Someone screamed horribly. It was not him.

The black powder smoke cleared, and Hardiman saw the ex-sheriff cradling his left arm against his chest. There was a greasy bloody stump where the old man's hand had been. The ill-used revolver lay in the dirt, and a big gritty cloud of black-powder smoke mushroomed up from it.

The bullet's charge had been too great for the age-fatigued rust-rotted metal. The chamber under the hammer had blown out and fired off the two adjacent chambers. The top half of the cylinder and frame was gone, and what was left was jagged orange-glowing scrap steel.

And the explosion had blown the ex-sheriff's good hand to hell.

Blood dribbled from the point of Hardiman's cheek. A piece of shattered gun frame had cut a three-inch gash from one ear nearly to the corner of his mouth. As cuts went, it was pretty bad, but it would not nearly kill him.

Hardiman felt like he'd been suspended three feet in the air and his boots were only now touching back down. He moved automatically, as if someone else were working his strings. After he tied the ex-sheriff's neckerchief tight around his lower arm, Hardiman got the old man under his arms and dragged him out to the main street. He mopped the extra blood from his cheek with his own neckerchief, then held it up against the cut to keep it from giving ideas to the men and a few women who came running. But they were purely interested in the show of the ex-sheriff's bloody stump, and no one paid the vaguest mind to Hardiman as he got his horse and rode away from there, fast as he could without looking back, as if he were running for his life.

Which he was, in a way. Soon as he was into the countryside, Hardiman slid out of the saddle—fell, almost— and sprawled out in the brown grass. His heart was slapping against his breastbone, his face was glazed with chill sweat, and he could not draw enough breath into his lungs. He dragged himself to a sitting position, drew up his knees and dropped his head between them, and stayed like that for the ten minutes it took for the shock to pass.

He pretended it was the cut and the loss of blood, but it wasn't and he knew it. It was fear, pure and crystalline as cold-spring water.

Oddly enough, once he'd recognized it, Hardiman was pretty much okay and saw how it was. The bleeding had mostly stopped, and Hardiman rode on until after nightfall, circling around the first five towns. He rode into the sixth, rousted a surgeon, and got his cheek stitched up. He spent the next week gathering money from the places he had cached it over the years, and then he rode north.

Here Chi stopped and stared across the table at Stern as if expecting comment, and getting none, she stared at her glass for a time. When she looked up, Stern was smiling as if he knew a secret.

Chi frowned. "He went to Waterloo, Iowa," she said, "and took up farming. Corn and hogs. Maybe he is there today, plowing and hoeing and slopping those swine. That surgeon was good with a needle and thread, and Hardiman gets plenty of sun. The scar is old and faint now."

Stern clasped both hands around his glass and leaned forward, his head cocked confidently. "Listen," he said.

"Wait." Chi raised one finger, and Stern shut his mouth. She sensed he would not get it, and her hunches rarely failed her. But she had told him her story and must try one last time. "Hardiman *was* enchanted, all those years. He knew he could not be touched by any other man, and it was true."

"Bullshit," Stern said, but he kept his smile.

Chi shook her head vigorously. "He believed it—that was enough. Even the old ex-sheriff's gun could not shoot him down."

Stern started to shake his head. Chi stabbed at him with a forefinger. "But something—maybe the little piece of gun metal that grazed his cheek, maybe only the loud noise so close—something reached deep down inside him, way down into his guts, and uncovered the fear that he'd locked up there so many years before. Now he knew: Some time down the road—maybe not right away, but some time—a man would fire at him, and with the magic gone, Hardiman would be shot dead."

"Okay," Stern said.

"But that isn't it either," Chi said. "The point is that he could accept the change. For a time he was accustomed to being immortal, but then he got accustomed to being mortal after all. Fate stopped watching over him, so he took over the job himself."

"That's all of it?" Stern asked.

Pendejo, Chi thought. *A smug sharper son of a bitch who would not know how to act if God himself demanded he be a man.* She tried to sit on her anger, but it was rising like beer in a spigot.

"Hey," Stern said softly, recognizing it. "Take it easy." One hand came away from his drink and eased across the table like a lizard. It touched lightly at her. Chi did not pull away, so Stern took her hand.

"That's why you sat here listening to me all afternoon," Chi said. "So you could hold my hand."

"Actually," Stern said, "no."

Chi drank down her last drink.

"Hand holding isn't what I have in mind," Stern said.

"Which is?"

"You know." Stern's smile got broad and lewd. "Sure you do."

Chi took a drag on her cigarette and ground it into the back of Stern's hand, at the webbing between the middle and ring fingers. Stern bleated like a goat and jerked his hand back. He stared at her furiously.

Chi watched him as if he were a spinning roulette wheel and she had money on the red. *If he does not say it*, she thought, *I will let it go*.

Stern rubbed at the little circle of burn, his eyes coring into her. Chi watched with fascination. He would not be able to stop himself—not unless he looked at her closely enough to see what could happen.

"You bitch," Stern said in a low hard voice.

Chi grabbed the edge of the table and tipped it over into Stern's lap. He was thrown backward, and his chair rose on two legs and toppled, dumping him onto the sawdusted floor. By then Chi was on her feet and around to him. She kicked him in the face, and when he covered it with his forearms, she kicked him in the stomach, and then she kicked him twice in the ribs.

The bartender was touching her arm. Chi spun around and half raised a hand, and though his shiny fat cheeks lost some color, the little man did not flinch from her. "Hey, now," he said, in a voice soft and expressionless enough to cut through the tequila and shame her.

Stern's nose was broken. There was blood all over his lips and chin and he was making bubbly sobbing sounds. He stared up at her through his tears in shock and bewilderment.

"That wasn't right," the bartender said in his soft voice.

Chi drew a deep shuddering breath. She reached under her serape, came out with a fistful of loose greenbacks, and held them out. When the bartender did not take them, she threw them at his feet. He wore black laced shoes shined to an ebony luster.

Her shoulder hit the doorjamb when she went out, and she had to think a moment about which way to turn. She hated every one of them at that moment but none more than herself.

Chapter Three

CORD OPENED HIS EYES SLOWLY AND CARE-
fully so he would not jar himself or irritate what felt
at that moment like a terribly fragile world. He was lying
on his back, naked between clean cotton sheets; their touch
was cool and slightly abrasive against his bare skin. He felt
the weight of a light blanket atop him, and his head was
cushioned deep in a feather-stuffed pillow.

Around him was neatness, order, and the trappings of
genteel living. This bedroom was decorated carefully as a
stage set. The bed had a head-and-foot piece of brass, a
good firmly ticked mattress, and sat high off the waxed-
and-polished hardwood floor. A subdued brown hemp oval
throw rug covered the center of the floor.

Across the room, on the wall to one side of the door,
was a three-quarter-length mirror. Cord tried to shift to a

position where he could see into it. The movement was not without pain.

His head ached beyond reach of the worst hangover, with a deep insistent pulsing throb that was enough to freeze him, propped on one elbow and balanced carefully against motion. Concentrating on himself in that position, eyes half-closed, he became aware that his right hand was wrapped in swathing. He opened his eyes again in a hurry.

It looked like he was wearing a mitten on his gun hand. Here was a new and disturbing experience, unprecedented in twenty years of mortal dependence on the assurance that a gun, and the skill and willingness to use it, was a thought away.

Cord stilled himself with effort. A fireplace was set into the wall to his left, with a tall, freestanding oak wardrobe standing alongside. To his right was a flattop desk with three drawers down one side and a straight-backed chair, and above the desk a white cabinet on which someone had taken some care to paint, freehand, a knobbed staff with wings at its top and two snakes twined around its shaft—a caduceus, a physician's symbol.

Two oil paintings hung to either side of the desk, landscapes in simple wooden frames. Each treated the same yellow-brown sweep of plains grass, with sharp-peaked mountains rising into the sky beyond, country like the basin.

Windows draped in lace curtaining flanked the bed. On a night table to Cord's left sat a reading lamp, a water glass and pitcher, and his watch. A second chair sat close by, facing the bed. His gun and clothes were nowhere evident.

Cord got himself painfully to a sitting position. The watch was stopped at 10:03. Cord turned it over and found a deep dent in the back of the case. The stem spun loosely between his fingers, and when he shook it, the works rattled. That figured.

Using the chair, Cord made it to his feet, grunting. His ankle was sprained, and he lurched to one side as he made for the wardrobe. He managed to get there without falling on his face. Inside he found only his boots and hat. He touched absently at his head and got another shock. Cord went to the mirror. An egg-sized patch of hair above his temple had been shaved down to the scalp and bandaged.

Cord stared at his naked body in the glass, the dressings on his hand and head—and around his neck, a rope burn, nothing deeply marked, just a ragged reddening, but enough to remind him of what had happened. With all his cuts and bruises and bandages, he looked like a newspaper caricature. But it was not so funny.

He was in strange territory, his weapons missing, and worst of all, he was debilitated in frightening ways. If someone were to come after him, he had nothing with which to defend himself and could not run. He tried the door. It was not locked.

He stood for a time with his hand on the knob, but he was beginning to sway unsteadily. The pain in his head was awful. He climbed back onto the bed. He was not going anywhere, not just yet.

Cord eased back and tried to absolutely clear his mind. Think nothing, he thought, and the ache will go away. What the hell can they do to you? The door latch clicked, and the door began to ease open, as if someone was concerned about waking him, just looking in.

Or slipping into position for a clean shot.

Cord lay quiet. What could he do?

The door swung full open and a handsome woman stood looking at him. Cord was pleased to be looking back. This woman was about Cord's age, tall and healthy-looking, with very dark hair done up on her head, dark eyes, and cleanly delineated features. Something in her face or expression struck Cord as smart, or skeptical, or merely amused— anyway, here was a woman who would brook no nonsense, but she might be willing to listen to sense. She wore a cardigan sweater over a dress and had good sturdy hips and a fine rise of breast. The earpieces of a stethoscope were hooked around her neck, connected by rubber tubing to the transmitter piece, which sat in the pocket of the sweater.

"Where's my revolver?" Cord demanded.

"Whom do you wish to shoot?" the woman asked coolly.

Some sons of bitches who tried to hang me dead, Cord almost said. But it seemed best to keep quiet until he got a sense of the wind's direction in these parts and who sided with which.

"Why don't you start over?" the woman said wryly. "Try this: 'Where am I?'"

"Enterprise, is my guess," Cord said, thinking out loud. It was the only town within fifty miles of where he'd been dropped, according to that barroom map that had set him out on this jaunt. "How did I get here?"

"I don't know," the woman said blandly. "I found you on my door stoop, like a basket of kittens no one wanted." She came over and sat in the chair beside the bed. "This is the surgery."

"Where's the doctor?" Cord asked.

"I'm the doctor. My name is Fiona Cobb."

Cord was pretty sure she was having him on, but his head hurt too much to make an issue of it.

"Give me your hand, Mister Cord."

Cord gave her a questioning look. "You know me?"

Fiona Cobb shook her head no. "Not before last night."

"See here," Cord said. "Who brought me to this place?"

She sobered, pursed her lips. She seemed about to answer, but then she shook her head slightly instead, as if to discourage him from pursuing the subject.

Cord did feel a little weary for this game at the moment. He settled for, "Where are my clothes?"

"Being washed. Don't worry, it won't do them any permanent damage." She leaned forward in the chair. "Give me your hand."

Cord did it. She cradled his hand in her lap palm up and began to unwrap the bandage. Cord felt the warmth of her thighs through the material of her dress and became aware of her odor. He thought at first it was medicine and then recognized it for whiskey. There was whiskey on this woman's breath. Cord wondered if the doctor knew his nurse was nipping at the medicinal alcohol.

"How does your head feel?" she asked as she unraveled gauze wrapping.

"It hurts."

She glanced up at him. "I'll bet it does."

Cord stared with dismay when the last of the dressing came off his hand. His palm and the insides of his fingers were flannel-red and raw, and covered with open blisters.

Fiona Cobb frowned. Cord closed his eyes so he would not have to look at his damaged hand and saw the big dark man named Bliss cutting the rope with his saber and then the flaming beam falling toward him. As he passed out he must have pushed it aside, his hand closing over the glowing char. He imagined the odor.

Fiona Cobb went to the cabinet decorated with the caduceus and returned with a roll of fresh bandages and a jar of some sort of ointment. The sight of his half-cooked hand was making Cord nauseous. "How long?" he croaked.

She rubbed cool ointment into his palm. "A day or two," she said. "It's a deep burn, and it will surely become infected if it is not kept medicated and bandaged until the sores scab over."

"Where's the doctor?" Cord demanded.

"*I'm* the doctor." She finished her bandaging. "So if it does become infected, I'll be the one to cut it off."

"Jesus," Cord said. "That's not a pretty thing to say."

"What else hurts?" Fiona Cobb said briskly.

"Twisted my ankle," Cord said. She pulled back the blanket and sheet in one long swift motion and leaned forward in the chair to probe at the joint with careful fingers.

"Minor sprain. Good as new in a day or two."

Fiona Cobb pulled the bedclothes back up over him. Her smile was a foot from his, and he felt her cool fingers trace the faint line of rope burn around his throat. That was how they were when the door opened.

The man who came through it was about Cord's age, though his hair was fine and beginning to thin. He wore dark britches, shoes, a dark vest over a white shirt, no collar or hat. He shut the door, leaned back against the mirror with his arms folded across his chest, gave Cord the once-over, and nodded. He looked a little smart-assed for Cord's mood, as if he were checking out a new rooster in the barnyard and deciding that the threat was minimal.

Fiona Cobb drew back her hand and sat up straight. She turned and looked at the man blankly.

"Are you the doctor?" Cord asked.

The man nodded in Fiona Cobb's direction. "She's the doctor," he said. "I'm the librarian."

All rightee, Cord thought. That made about as much sense as any of this.

Fiona Cobb got up from the chair and went back to the

cabinet. "This is Richard Carlisle," she said. She replaced the ointment and got out a bottle of whiskey. "Richard, meet Mister Cord." She gestured with the bottle.

"I know who you are," Carlisle said to Cord.

"Everyone does," Cord snapped. "People bandy my name all over the damned place."

"Your reputation precedes you," Carlisle suggested.

"Tell me something new." Cord winced with the pain of sitting up in bed. "What is going on in this basin?"

"You mean," Richard Carlisle said, "why weren't you killed?"

Fiona Cobb took two water tumblers from a desk drawer and poured a couple of fingers of whiskey into each. She carried one over to Carlisle, who was watching Cord with a sort of superior smirk.

Cord scowled back. This hombre seemed to know some things, and Cord figured the woman did as well. The doctor; imagine that.

"Last night," Cord said, "I saw a mob lynch a man."

"A rustler," Carlisle said.

"He said he wasn't."

Carlisle nodded thoughtfully, as if this added a new, theoretical dimension to the discussion. Dr. Fiona Cobb stood with one arm across her chest and the other holding her whiskey just below her chin, looking from Carlisle to her patient. "The circumstantial evidence was against him," Carlisle said. "And stealing stock is a hanging offense in this basin."

"What the hell are you talking about?" Cord looked to Fiona Cobb but got only a neutral blank stare back. "Listen closely: Not so long ago, somewhere near to here, a bunch of masked night-riding hoodlums hanged a man dead. Is that within the law in these parts?"

"Not within the letter," Fiona Cobb said to her whiskey, "but within the spirit."

"We do not need law," Carlisle said. "We have Mallory Bliss."

"I knew the man they hanged," Cord said.

Fiona Cobb laughed abruptly and went to the window. But Carlisle was frowning. "Not to put too fine a point on it, but I wouldn't go abroad mourning your old friend out loud."

"He was no friend," Cord said. "His name was Wee Bill Blewin, and he was something of a bad hand in some ways. He has stolen plenty enough in his days, including horses and cows, could be. Maybe he's killed men, though I doubt it. But for what he was accused of last night by that mass of renegades," Cord said, "could be they hanged an innocent man."

"Figure his accumulated sins caught up with him," Carlisle said, "and thank your stars you did not share his fate."

Arguing had turned up the pounding in Cord's head. "How about a taste of that whiskey, Carlisle?"

Carlisle shook his head no. "It might run counter to doctor's orders, Mister Cord. We can't take chances in your delicate condition."

"You ever hear of civility?" Cord snapped.

Carlisle shrugged and sucked at his drink.

Fiona Cobb was filling a third glass. "It would be best if you accepted our situation. We must live here." She turned to face Cord. "There is no trouble in Basin County."

"There will be," Cord snarled. "Soon as I get well enough, I'm going to make some. Just for the exercise."

Fiona Cobb handed Cord the glass. "You are delirious," she said. "So be careful what you say."

Cord was too hurt and tired to deal with this nonsense

right now. "That's right," he said. "I am crazy as six Swedes." He took a big slug from the glass and gagged. Its contents, though alcoholic, were definitely not whiskey. "What is this?"

"Laudanum," Fiona Cobb said.

"Laudanum!" Cord echoed. "That will curdle your brains."

The doctor laughed. "Then you have nothing to worry about, Mister Cord."

It did seem to help with the pain. Cord drank again.

"He will be fit as a fiddle now," Carlisle said.

"Get out of here, Richard," Fiona Cobb said, watching Cord drink.

"Wait a minute." Maybe it was the laudanum, but Cord had a hunch. He looked past the door. "You know who brought me in here."

Carlisle shrugged. "Someone found you on the trail. Think of him as an anonymous benefactor."

Cord shook his head. "I don't like owing someone I don't know. I am going to find some things out."

"You've already spent more luck than most men get," Carlisle said seriously. "Soon as you are well, ride on."

"Let men handle me that way and walk on away?" Cord said with rich scorn. "When pigs fly," he spit.

"Go now, Richard," Fiona Cobb said more gently. Carlisle gave Cord a different, more thoughtful look, then did as he was told.

Cord watched him go. "Mallory Bliss." Cord spat out the name and felt himself going goofy. "Fix his wagon." Fiona Cobb sat in the chair beside his bed and watched him placidly, sipping at her drink. His face felt strange and he had the notion he was grinning oafishly. "Tear his ears off and feed them to the hogs," he said thickly.

"Good idea."

"Make him bellycrawl and eat dirt."

"Whatever you say." She placed her palm on his forehead. "Take a break, Mister Cord," she said softly. "Go away for a while."

She went on murmuring, and her hand felt cool and dry. Cord drifted down to laudanum sleep and for a few moments saw Chi smiling at him in the sunlight with willows somewhere behind her, before he was altogether gone.

Two days back, riding north along the Yellowstone and out of Paradise Valley, Cord and Chi had reached the little Montana railroad town of Livingston. There was where it had properly begun, in the midafternoon of a fine bright day.

Cord pressed for getting a bite to eat and pushing on for Bozeman. They had a half-dozen hours of daylight left, he argued, and they could camp on the trail. He'd feel best after they'd laid some distance between them and recent trouble.

There had been killing in Paradise Valley, of the particularly mean and pointless sort that Cord found monstrously unsettling of late. Ironically, the best man in the whole mixup had died of natural causes—if you could call something like cancer natural. To Cord, the notion of cells running wild and eating your body from the inside out was about as natural as a two-headed calf.

That man was named Arrowsmith, and long ago, back beyond the ten years that Cord and Chi had been together, she and Arrowsmith had been partners. Cord knew the old man's death had shaken Chi deeply and took it as the reason she had been so moody and touchy and silent. Cord had mellowed some over the years and could be patient with her.

So he had time to think on the trail and found himself wondering whether he was turning irresolute, keeping his peace and abiding just to keep her gentle. He decided to believe instead that he was merely practicing the art of getting along, of balancing outlaw inclinations against citizeny aspirations. He had to learn some new tricks if there were a chance of them settling together.

Whatever the reasons, Cord kept his trap shut and let her have her head for the nonce. Their goal was the Bitter Root Valley a couple hundred miles west and across the divide. They'd been heading for that country for some time now, and this was the closest they'd managed to get, so Cord was anxious that no moodiness or any trouble slow or detour them. He was entertaining notions of joining the squirearchy.

For a good long time it had been hard enough to get Chi to even consider the idea of turning their money into ranchland. Then the introduction of each successive step in his daydream met renewed resistance, most lately the details of the two of them together in a radically new sort of partnership. But over time his running on forced her to consider. She still hadn't given him any good ideas about her feelings on coming into his bed, but other things she said indicated she had come to accept that their back roads were vanishing into settlements.

So these days he worked on convincing her that owning acreage was the only route to real freedom. Without their own land there was no telling what awful ways they might be forced to go to ground.

Anyway, there in Livingston, Cord was for a quick supper and moving on, but Chi said no, she was going to do some drinking. They ended at a hole-in-the-wall saloon called the Bijou, a few doors up a side street near the railroad switch-yards. It was a dirty, ill-lit place with a trestle bar, three tables, one filthy window, and a revolving clientele of brake-men and engineers coming off the day shift or bracing for the night shift.

Cord had been hoping for a beefsteak, fried potatoes, and a sliced tomato broiled with cheese, but he settled for a cold ham sandwich and a hard-boiled egg. Chi started right in on a bottle of tequila.

At first she wouldn't talk at all, just stared sourly into her drink while Cord toyed with a bottle of beer. For near the first time he could remember, she was drunk in a hurry. "We don't get out of here, we're going to lose another day," Cord said when he noticed.

"Another day in 'our home country,'" Chi said sarcastically. "The wonderful Bitter Root Valley with Goodman Cord, the *hacendado*." She sipped at her tequila. "And what shall I be, Cord? Your woman? Your ranch wife?"

"Hey, now," Cord murmured, making the sort of meaningless soothing sounds he'd use on a jumpy horse. Only thing was, Chi, like this, was worse than any skittish animal. She was more like a mine tunnel full of gas, and everyone around lighting up smokes.

"Will I wear an apron?" Chi went on in that sour voice, "and cut my hair short?" She toyed unconsciously with one of her dark waist-length braids, twining it around her fingers. "How will I look to you in a bonnet and a crinoline dress and flour all over my hands? Is that my part in your fine dream, Cord?"

"What's eating you?"

"You are, *querido*." Her tone had turned real nasty. "You

and your pipe dreams, and your airs about turning into something you will never be."

"How's that?" Cord tried to keep his voice neutral.

"Mister Cord," Chi said in a low mocking voice. "You can't change what you are, Mister Cord. All the money you can ever steal, all the land you can fence, you'll still be the same as you were born."

"Which is?"

Chi leaned forward and smiled sweetly. "Texas dirt trash."

Cord snapped back as if slapped—and yet somehow, some way, he managed to keep a rein on himself. "We will talk some other time."

"Fine," Chi said amiably. "But I won't be any different, and neither will you."

Cord might have learned some new tricks about keeping his temper, but he would not stand for this mean bully-ragging, not in this life, so he excused himself. He wandered the town until dark. In other days he might have gotten drunk or into some other kind of childishness. But right now he just didn't feel like it, and finally there was nothing for it but to go to bed.

There he lay open-eyed and thought, what if she was right? Or worse, what if she simply could not manage the idea of bedding with only one man? It did not take much of that sort of musing to convince him that on this night there would be no sleep without whiskey, so he dressed and went down to the lobby. Across the street he could see Chi knocking back the tequila inside the Bijou Saloon. He did not want to face her again right then, so he gave the desk clerk a dollar to go get him a pint jug.

The desk clerk was a thin young bald man with a perpetual sneer, as if anyone who would stay in his hotel were beneath his social notice. When he came back with the bottle, his sneer had transmogrified into a smarmy grin. "Your lady friend is over there," he told Cord. "Having herself a time."

Cord stared at him. "All night long I have wanted to hit someone," he said. "Say one word more, and you are it."

Upstairs in bed, Cord sipped the whiskey and waited, but he did not hear her come back to the room next to his. For a long time he lay thinking angry thoughts, but by and by he fell away into fitful sleep and vague anxious dreams.

The next morning Cord stood awhile in the hallway outside Chi's door, considering the pluses and minuses of knocking. Ultimately he decided that waking her was dangerous. She was probably hung over.

Cord was not really hungry, but he killed some time in a café, drinking coffee and reading a two-day-old newspaper, hoping she would come along in a more cheerful humor, but trying mostly not to think about her. When he could not hold himself longer, he went back to the hotel. The clerk watched him come in, as if expecting this.

"Has she come down?" Cord asked.

"Who would that be?"

Cord pointed a finger at him. "Nope," the clerk said quickly, but then he got his lick in anyway. "She never went up."

Cord nearly lost his temper. "Tell it," he snapped.

"She checked out last night," the clerk said. "Somewhere around midnight. Had the boy fetch her gear and horse from the livery."

"How'd she seem?"

"Drunker than any woman I ever saw," the clerk said.

"She say anything?"

"Yeah," the clerk said. " '*Adios*.' "

Cord went up to his room. He rolled a cigarette and rested back on the bed, wondering if she had left him for good and for true. By the end of the cigarette, Cord knew such pondering would get him nowhere but crazy. Without thinking about it, he was off the bed and packing his bags, doing what he always did in times of uncertainty and trouble, moving on, out into the country.

He would circle up to the grazing prairies between the Missouri and Yellowstone rivers, take a look around. Maybe drink a cup of coffee with the big cattlemen and learn a thing or two about the ways of empire building.

Cord told the clerk he would return in one week. Meanwhile he would leave a note, in case the woman came looking for him.

"Think she will?" the clerk asked.

But Cord was tired of the man and busy pondering what to write. He dated the stationery and scrawled, "Gone north to see how the real cattle barons operate. Maybe they can teach me to wipe the horseshit off my boots before stepping on the carpet." She might think it funny, if she saw it.

Cord sealed the envelope with wax and gave it and five dollars to the clerk. "You aren't much in my eyes," he said to the clerk, "but I will wager you are man enough not to take money and then not do a thing."

"You are the trusting sort, mister."

"Uh-uh," Cord contradicted. "I am coming back, and I will know if you played me false. Guess what will happen then?"

The clerk stopped smiling. "Set your mind to ease, Mister."

"Why, thank you," Cord said broadly, "I'll do that."

A half hour later, Cord was riding north up the Shields River, feeling better already. As the territory opened up and

the settlements fell behind him, calm euphoria took over.
Cord felt fine, and went on feeling fine all that day, right
up until the time when some sons of bitches tried hanging
him dead.

The room was dark the next time Cord awoke, dark
except for the rectangle of the open door, and there she was:
her familiar silhouette framed there and backlit by yellow
light from the hallway, the drape of her serape and the flat
line of her sombrero. The other woman, the doctor, stood
behind, holding a lantern wicked down low. But deep shadows shrouded the bed where he lay, the darkness a palpable
weight upon him. His face was glazed with feverish sweat.

He tried to form his lips into the syllable of her name,
but they were fat and rubbery and would not work. Cord
stared across the vastness of the room and remembered the
laudanum. His tongue filled his mouth. The women were
talking: Cord could not make out the words, but their tones
were low and soothing. He could sink back into sleep's
embrace and be safe. Cord felt like a child and liked the
feeling fine.

Then her face, half-lit by the lantern, hovered above him.
She said his name in a low soft voice. "Drunk again, *querido?*" she asked. Her voice was musical and teasing.

Cord opened his mouth and someone put a bottle to his
lips. Cord gagged down another draught of the laudanum.

A cool hand touched a cloth to his forehead and swabbed
away sweat. Cord suddenly shook with night chills, but it
broke him loose from the laudanum's grip for a moment
and he made out her face clearly before it moved up and
away.

"Hey," Cord said thickly. *"Que pasa?"*

She said something. Her tone was sweet and narcotic

like the laudanum and started to take him away again. He closed his fat clumsy lips and dropped his heavy eyelids.

He thought she kissed him on the forehead just as he drifted back into sleep. It was a nice idea anyway, and he carried it with him when he redescended into laudanum peace.

Chapter Four

THIS TIME THERE WAS SUNLIGHT, BRIGHTLY filtering through the curtains, warm where it touched Cord's skin. Cord looked around, and there was Chi, real as the world could ever be.

She had pulled the chair over near to the desk so she could lean back against the wall. Her chin was tipped forward to her chest, so the brim of her sombrero concealed her face, and her hands were hidden under her serape. As always, she wore the black leather britches tucked into the high tooled uppers of her black boots. The two long black braids of hair trailed down over her shoulders, shining against the serape's rough wool.

She could have been dozing, but she stirred as soon as his gaze touched her. The front legs of the chair touched down on the flooring, and she raised her head to show him her handsome brown face lit with a smile, like daylight breaking over the horizon. "Not dead, eh?" she said.

He thought he should perhaps be angry. The last time they'd been face-to-face she'd spit some hard bad news at him; now she was playing jokes as if that behavior had never been. But the truth of it was, the anger was simply not there. He was just damned pleased to see her. Here she was, with him once more, and Cord was relieved as a cub.

"*Como está?*" she asked.

"*Asi asi.*"

"Good enough." Chi tipped back her hat brim. "You feel like eating something?"

Soon as she suggested it, Cord was suddenly and ravenously hungry. He took that as a good sign; he had always associated appetite with health and healing. "Fine idea." No one had dressed him, and he stayed where he was. "How long have I been out?"

"Two nights and day, *la médica* told me." Chi gave him a critical once-over. "It looks as if she fixed you up all right."

Cord showed her his bandaged right hand. "*Más o menos.*" He wondered how she'd found him, and why she'd come looking in the first place, but there was time for all of that, now she was here. The thought of food was making him salivate. "My clothes in that wardrobe?" It embarrassed him somewhat to be naked with her there, even if he were covered with a sheet and blanket.

Chi jutted her chin in the direction of the wardrobe. "Take a look." She was getting a big kick out of this.

"Right." Cord stayed where he was. "You want to kind of get out of here?"

"No," Chi said. "I want to watch."

"Well you can't," Cord said.

"Too bad." Chi stood, stretched langorously, and went

to the door. "I kind of had my heart set on it. That's what I was hanging around for." She opened the door. "Actually," she added. "I peeked under the covers while you were sleeping." And out she went, leaving Cord to gape at the closed door.

Cord got out of the bed carefully. The ache in his head was dull and distant and had more to do with hunger and opium hangover than injury, he decided. The bandage had been removed to give the head wound air, and in the mirror he saw that it was healing nicely. He could walk normally without the sprained ankle giving him more than a twinge. As for the rope burn, it was just livid enough to remind him that soon as he got some food and answers, he might have to see some people.

That brought him to the most worrisome problem: the gun hand, still mittened up in gauze. He went to the wardrobe, thinking how you took blessings like two good hands for granted until you lost them. His clothing was neatly folded on a shelf in the closet—union suit, socks, britches, shirt, vest, hat—and surprisingly, his belt and holster, with his gun where it belonged. Resting atop the pile was the tobacco pouch Chi had run off with back in Livingston.

Cord dressed awkwardly, working around the bandaged hand. When he was finished, he stood there regarding himself in the mirror, getting back into the man he was. After a time he removed his Stetson again, stared at the cut as he fingered the little ridge of puckered skin. His hand was tender beneath the dressing. These stigmata bothered him in a practical sense, but there was more to it: he blanched to see the visible marks of his infirmity, the mortal weakness he wished to deny. Only lately, deep in himself, Cord had begun to give credence to an old suspicion that he was simply not as tough—physically or mentally—as he had been in the old hell-bent-for-trouble outlaw days. No one was, in this new world where cancer could ambush you sure as guns.

Not that guns weren't a concern as well. Should he need to use his Colt—and likely he would, if he stayed long in this basin—he would have to go at it left-handed. Cord slipped his holster off the belt and repositioned it on the opposite side, then stood before the three-quarters-length mirror and took a try at drawing left-handed.

Years back Cord had taken some serious gunfighter lessons from a legendary shootist named J.W. Baron. Cord had run across Baron in Abilene, Kansas, at the end of what turned out to be Cord's last cattle drive up from south Texas. Baron counseled ambidextrousness. It was a contingency you might never in your life use, but in the case of some difficulty with your regular gun arm, it could save your life. Survival had been J.W. Baron's specialty—until he'd been back-shot in the barnyard of a northern Nevada ranch. Cord was there when it happened.

But Cord had learned to shoot at least 95 percent as good with his left as his right and kept up the practice for years, until not so long ago, easing off when he and Chi became regular citizens. Still, there in front of the mirror, the move wasn't too bad after a couple of tries: smooth, if a little slow. He might even be able to hit something, if he had to. If he had the time.

Chi was leaning against the hallway wall when Cord came out, her arms folded under her serape. The door opposite opened on an examining room. "You doing okay?" Chi asked.

"Huh?" He was surprised by her solicitousness.

"I would have hated it, riding all this way to find you

dead." But it didn't come out as lightly as she meant to make it.

"Looks like you got lucky." He was always edgy when he was not sure of her mood. "How about that breakfast?" He looked back out the window at the sunshine. "It is morning, right?"

But she stayed where she was, studying the floor. "What I said. The last time I saw you."

Her discomfiture discomfited him; the habit of avoiding intimate revelations, though changing, was still a deep part of him, an instinctive protective response.

"All this talk about land buying and stock growing and settling in like bears for a forever winter." Chi looked up at him. "I felt like I was being treed, and I got . . . dismayed."

"*Dismayed*," Cord echoed. "Panicked is more like it."

"Listen, Cord," Chi said firmly. "I am not used to being scared. I never could afford the luxury. I found myself backed up into that cave you've been trying to carve for me, and I wanted daylight, and quick. I thought I couldn't breathe." She shook her head, impatient with herself. "Maybe I was too quick with my claws."

Cord worried the edge of the bandage around his right hand. Both of them worked hard to make the lives they wished, but she had to work harder. A lot of it had to do with her being a woman.

Long ago Chi had stepped outside society's preconceptions of women's ways, and it cost her. A lot of women regarded her as if she were deformed; too many men saw her as a character in their perverse fantasies. And when those sort of people tried to mold her into *their* idea of how *she* should be, she had damned little patience for any of it. Who could blame her?

Maybe that was how she had come to see Cord lately, since he'd been blathering on about settling in, and living easy on some piece of Montana bottomland: another meddler trying to manipulate her. Maybe she thought he was casting her in the make-believe story of his own safe-assed future. But then again, she was here, wasn't she?

Cord looked up and Chi was grinning tentatively, as if waiting for him to make the next move. Damned if he knew what; trying to figure out the right thing to say was making him sweaty.

"Think you can try putting up with me again?" Chi asked.

"Got to," Cord muttered. "You're all I got." He meant to make it sound like a joke, but it came out serious to his ears. He thought of something to do. "I got to go kill a snake," he said and turned for the back door.

Chi put her hand on his arm. He stopped.

"Well, I'm sorry," Chi said firmly, almost with irritation. "That's all."

To Cord's disquietude was added astonishment: in all their time together he had never known her to apologize, to him or anybody. How the hell was her mind running these days? Cord wondered on it in slippery bewilderment and then gave it up. She was complex in ways he could only compare to a cut diamond, glittering here and then there, always clear at the center and always changing with the light.

One thing was certain: If they ever did make a settled man-and-woman life together, it would rarely be routine.

"Try not to do it again," Cord said, kind of gruff and mostly interested in getting away.

Cord passed the open door of Fiona Cobb's bedroom. The hall ended at a sitting room facing the front of the house. Cord turned the other way, passed through a kitchen, and went out to the backyard.

A hot blast of wind hit him in the face as he stepped out; the weather had taken an odd turn in the time he'd been out, the air much too warm and dry for this time of the year. Cord faced into the breeze and headed for the privy, wading through a few chickens pecking in the patch turned for a kitchen garden. An irrigation ditch had been cut to run along one side and the back line of Fiona Cobb's lot; Cord looked upstream and saw a tall windmill above roofs of town buildings in the north. On the far side of the ditch was a line of cottonwood saplings, the beginning of a wind-break.

Way off west toward the divide, the snow line had already moved halfway up the mountains. But against the north side of the little privy building, a bank of dirty old snow remained, drifted high as a man's waist.

A long blanket-wrapped bundle had been laid atop the snowpile, and more snow packed up along its sides. Cord worked loose a flap of the wool and looked into the gray face of Wee Bill Blewin.

His mouth was open and his cheek was smeared with soot, and the closed lids of his eyes were coated with frost. Cord stared down into the face for a long moment before he turned away. A body stored for keeping in a doctor-woman's snowbank. To hell with all of them. This would work out. Chi was back, over her drunk and her mad, and she wouldn't let him get into anything *too* blockheaded.

He found Chi waiting in the front yard. From that vantage this was a pretty little place, with a white picket fence surrounding grass spring-green from the ditch water. A pole rising from the gatepost supported a shingle: FIONA COBB, M.D.

"We will walk," Chi announced. Cord held the gate for her and she said, "*Gracias*," almost gaily.

But Cord, though he was hungry and feeling himself once more, and relieved that they were teamed up again, was not nearly as gay. The hanging and burning of Wee Bill Blewin was haunting him—dead is dead, but somehow in this case it was more horrible for the method.

Maybe he was simply irritated beyond distraction. Cord was not so quick to think vengeance as in earlier days, but there were some varieties of trashy carryings-on he would not abide. He could not afford to, not if he wished to ever again think anything of himself. "All right," he said to Chi. "Lead on. Likely you already know your way around."

For the moment this town looked calm as daisies. Fiona Cobb's surgery was on a side street that formed the stubby southerly foot of an L with the main business district. Vacant lots lined the rest of her street; this residential fringe of Enterprise had been surveyed and platted, but there were no signs of residents besides Dr. Cobb and Richard Carlisle, here or anywhere else in town.

"How'd you know I was here?" Cord said.

"I saw your horse, so I made inquiries."

"My horse?"

"In the livery corral," Chi said with some impatience. Cord thought he saw a touch of color high up on her cheek. "I got your note," she said, "once I'd sobered up. I guess I know you well enough to track you down."

"You know what happened?" Cord asked her.

"I've got an idea." Chi smiled. "From the looks of you, you ran into some trouble. Unless you got drunk and rode over a cliff."

"I might have to see to business here before we ride on," Cord said carefully, trying the notion out on her.

"Well, sure," Chi said, as if it were already decided. "I'll be siding you." She flashed him a quick grin. "That ranch in the Bitter Root will wait for us." Cord was about to make a remark, but then they turned onto the main street.

Bliss Basin was open range in every direction, broken only by a few rolling hills one way, a meandering line of cottonwoods marking a creek another way, the whole great bowl rimmed by mountains. In the center of this unspoiled wilderness sat Enterprise, like a seat of permanence and modern refinements.

The stage road here became the town's main street, one good-sized block long. Everything was neat and spruce and looked to have been built recently. By whom? Cord wondered, and why? This Enterprise looked to have amenities and ambitions. Yet there was not a soul in sight.

To Cord's right as they walked on down the street, a good-sized two-story building was identified by a nicely painted sign as the Enterprise House. A café and a saloon occupied either side of the first floor; the second story was topped by a squared false front, while a balcony fronted the curtained windows of a couple of hotel rooms. Here was home, Cord thought. It seemed like half his life had been spent in such rooms.

Past an alley was the mercantile, a one-story building with two plate-glass windows. In a high-roofed open-fronted storage shed behind it, heavy rolling stock farming equipment was on display: two giant iron-wheeled Case steam tractors getting a bit rusty in the remnants of drifted snow, a half-dozen horse-drawn mowing machines with their five-foot sickle bars pointing to the roof, a dozen of those fine new dump hay rakes. Cord wished he had been here to see the Case tractors arrive; someone had to have driven them overland from the railhead, hundreds of miles at two or three miles in an hour. It must have taken weeks.

Some new tack, harness and the like, was draped over a rack at the back of the shed. Everything was left out in the open; there must have been damned little crime in this town. Beyond the mercantile sat a livery barn. Cord's gelding and Chi's mare were in the corral out back.

The buildings on the west side of the street were even more solid and permanent-looking. The one at the south end had two main chambers, the near one of wood, the far one built of gray-brown granite blocks mortared with cement. The near part was topped by a small steeple with an open top containing a bell: a church, Cord thought, until he noted behind it a run of seesaws and swings, neatly painted and maintained. It was a school. Meaning there had to be children in these parts, which in turn meant there were families. Well, maybe, Cord thought, though he was beginning to wonder where they lived.

The schoolhouse was attached to the granite building, which was fronted by its own entrance up three stone steps. Carved in the lintel, a solid slab of granite, was the legend, in heavy Roman letters: ENTERPRISE FREE LIBRARY. Cord recalled Richard Carlisle, calling himself the librarian; at the time Cord had figured it for a stupid joke. Further on up the street was a square one-story building constructed of red brick, whose sign identified it as the Territorial Bank of Enterprise.

Beyond the last buildings, where the street again became a rough range road, stood the windmill Cord had spotted from Fiona Cobb's backyard. The road split to pass it on either side; the windmill towered over the town like a sentinel. It was a good hundred feet high, with a ladder climbing one side of the enclosed framework. The wheel at its top was many-veined and a good ten feet across and spinning now in the warm morning breeze from the mountains off west. The two ditches branched off through headgates from the holding tank at the windmill's foot.

Beside it was parked an excavator ditch-digging machine. Cord had heard of them but never seen one up close, with its metal cups running on an endless chain. Cord marked it up. Before he left this town he was going to have a close look at this machine. Could be something he'd want to own one day not so distant.

Still, there was something distinctly eerie about this fine modern empty town in the middle of nowhere. Some years back, at the opera house in Leadville, Colorado, Cord had seen a performance of *The Flying Dutchman*, and this Enterprise reminded him of the shade of Wagner's Captain Vanderdecken, condemned to round the Cape of Good Hope forever—alone, and to no point.

Then, standing there in the middle of this town gone ghost too soon, Cord spotted smoke rising from the café's chimney and shook off his musings. He followed Chi up on the boardwalk and under the painted sign, blinking for a moment as his eyes dilated in the cool dimness.

Here was a neat, clean, little place, the sort of establishment whose appointments suggested that breakfasting would be a pleasant pastime. The wooden floor was swept clean around half a dozen matching rectangular tables with two or four or six chairs, arranged about a cold cast-iron furnace stove. In the back corner a door connected with the saloon, and nearby a half-counter service window separated the kitchen from the dining area. Cord heard the sizzle of cooking coming from that precinct, and the aroma of coffee and food sharpened his hunger.

Fiona Cobb looked up and said, "Join me, please." She

sat alone at one of the tables and seemed genuinely pleased to see Cord, her patient, up and hale. The table was spread with a tablecloth and set with white cups and saucers decorated with graceful scrolling, with carefully laid silver flatware to either side. Fiona Cobb nodded civilly, even pleasantly, to Chi. Cord noted it as a courteous gesture and wondered dimly what had already passed between the two women and if they had discovered some things they had in common.

Richard Carlisle came from the kitchen with a pot of coffee and a mostly full bottle of whiskey. "Back from the dead, I see," he said to Cord. Cord didn't rise to the gibe; he was tired of that sort of scratching match. What he wanted was food. Carlisle set the pot and the bottle on the table and returned to the kitchen.

Fiona Cobb poured coffee all around. "How do you feel?" While she asked, she put a dollop of whiskey into her cup and the one at Carlisle's place, the move unselfconscious, as if first-thing-in-the-morning drinking was a normal and unremarkable routine for the two of them.

"I'm okay," Cord said. He gestured with his bandaged hand. "This bothers me."

"Time heals all wounds," Fiona Cobb said.

"Then we shouldn't ought to need doctors," Cord said.

She laughed. "Too late for you now, Cord," she said. "You've already had my treatment."

Carlisle returned with a tray of four plates and dealt them out. Cord in his hunger was fairly overwhelmed: there were fried eggs, hot sliced beef with gravy, fried potatoes, canned peaches shiny with syrup, and thick slabs of coarse-grained wheat bread lathered with butter. Carlisle set the tray on a nearby table and joined them.

Cord tried the coffee. It was hot and dark and wonderful.

"What's your fee?" he asked the doctor, digging into his eating. "Never mind," he went on with his mouth full, "send your bill to Mallory Bliss. It was his night riders who tried to hang me."

That touched a sore nerve. Fiona Cobb held her laced coffee halfway to her mouth, and Carlisle pursed his lips in a tight thin line.

"Your argument might not be with Bliss," Carlisle said carefully.

"He'll do until someone else comes along." With each bite, Cord was feeling better. His left hand worked a fork pretty handily, it turned out.

"I was happy to minister to you, Mister Cord," Fiona Cobb said. She watched her plate, as if her eggs were watching back. "There is no charge." She looked at Carlisle.

"We've been talking," Carlisle said.

"Bet you have." Cord folded a buttered slice of bread in half and stuck it in his mouth.

"I wish to solicit your help," Fiona Cobb said. She looked from Cord to Chi to include her, but Chi seemed totally involved in her breakfast, as if she were not listening.

"You?" Cord asked.

"Us," Fiona Cobb emended. "We want to speak with you about a favor."

"More of a job, actually," Carlisle said. "There is money in it," he added, as if that cinched the deal.

Cord mopped up the last of his eggs with the last of his beef and stared down at his empty dish. "Guess I'm ahead of the rest of you." He gestured with his fork at Carlisle's plate. "You going to finish those eggs?"

Carlisle frowned. He took his napkin from his lap and placed it on the table, pushed his chair back. Fiona Cobb concentrated on eating, while Carlisle took Cord's plate to the kitchen and said nothing when he came back with seconds on everything and set the refilled plate before Cord. "You make a swell breakfast," Cord said. "I will say that." He hunkered down to some more serious eating.

But just as Cord lifted a forkful of beef and egg to his mouth, footsteps sounded on the plank walkway out front of the café. Cord put down the fork, adjusted his chair around and a little away from the table. Chi went on with her absorbed eating. The café door swung open to the morning, and a newcomer paused in the doorway, so anyone who wished could get a good look at him in full daylight. Cord sat chewing his beef, wondering if this should be cause for alarm and deciding not.

The fellow in the doorway was compact, wiry, a very fit fifty or so years old. Cord sensed toughness: not the gunhand sort, but rather the true thing derived from a lifetime at work on the land. He wore a slouch hat, checkered California pants, and was giving a thick cud of tobacco a real workout with a jaw square as a bookshelf. He stepped inside, closed the door against the flies, and stood studying them with a clear eye.

"Meet Mister F. X. Connaught." Carlisle smiled. "F. X., you probably know these two."

"F. X. is foreman to Mallory Bliss," Fiona Cobb said.

"Good for you," Cord said to Connaught. "What's your beef?"

Connaught kept his expression neutral.

"One thing more," Fiona Cobb said quickly. "You should know that F. X. was the one who brought you to me the night before last."

Cord turned in his chair. "You just remembered that?"

Fiona Cobb reddened slightly. "I didn't want to . . . trouble you while you were ill."

"You didn't want to be mouthing off," Cord suggested, "until you knew how mad I was, and at whom."

"St. Jerome writes that 'the scars of others should teach us caution,'" Carlisle said.

"Do give it a rest, Richard," Fiona Cobb snapped.

"Cord," Chi said.

"Huh?" He looked her way.

Chi pointed with her butter knife. "Your breakfast is getting cold."

Cord gawped at her. She smiled sweetly and went back to her eating. "Well, I don't like people standing around when I eat." Cord regarded Connaught. "You weren't with those lynchers the other night by any chance?"

Connaught made no response, but Cord knew Connaught had not been among the night riders. The sort of man who ran in an animal pack wouldn't likely have the sand to come in to face him alone, especially not now that Cord's name and repute seemed to have spread across the basin. And there was Chi's unconcern: her instinct stood for a lot. "Well, sit and take some coffee or eggs or something," Cord said.

The little dour black Irishman thought about it; likely he had not gotten this old in this country without exercising considerable caution. "Coffee," he decided, and drew a chair over.

"Wonderful," Cord said, and went back to his eating. Carlisle fetched a cup for Connaught and filled it and his own and Chi's. Chi pushed her empty plate aside, reached across the table, and took Cord's makings from his shirt pocket.

"You keep stealing that," Cord said mildly.

"Borrowing," Chi corrected. "That's why I ran you down, so you wouldn't remember me as the tobacco-thieving sort."

Fiona Cobb and Carlisle paid attention to their whiskey

and coffee and took care not to interrupt the banter. Having made their overture to Cord and Chi, the doctor and the librarian seemed suddenly leery of them. Connaught was silent and at apparent ease, satisfied to watch Chi's skilled fingers build cigarettes.

Cord wiped his plate clean with the last of his bread. "Now then," he said to Connaught. "How did you happen to end up my ambulance driver?"

"I follow the order of Mister Bliss," Connaught said, deadpan.

"All the time?"

Connaught drank some coffee. Here was a man for whom words had worth, and not the sort to give them away gratis.

"Okay," Cord said. "Where did you encounter my remains?"

"At the home place." Connaught watched Cord take the lit cigarette Chi offered. "There Mister Bliss asked me to fetch you to the doctor."

"How did I get hurt?"

"Mister Bliss said you fell from your horse."

Cord leaned across the table toward Connaught. "Sure I did," he said unpleasantly. "But first I hit myself over the head, stuck my hand in the campfire, and tried to hang myself."

Emotion flickered across Connaught's dour face. He knew the true facts right enough, Cord decided, and his loyalty to Bliss was tempered by some disapproval.

"Looks to me like lots of odd accidents happen around here," Cord went on harshly. "Just the other while ago I found a burned-up dead man in the snowbank out back of the surgery."

"I brought him in last night," Chi said. "It was too dark for burying." Chi blew a smoke ring and said, "I got a look at him, though," watching Cord in a way he suddenly disliked.

"Someone we once knew," he said evenly.

"Could be," Chi agreed.

From the corner of his eye, Cord caught a glimpse of Fiona Cobb watching curiously. She had caught the significance in Chi's tone. Cord wasn't much interested in what she thought, but he liked less that quick turn toward the dark in the look Chi held steady on him. Recognizing Wee Bill Blewin had recalled for her another man, and a bad time long before. Cord had been at the center of some mean trouble and had good reason subsequently to want to forget it. Right now she would not let him, and he even thought for a moment she meant to rehash it for everyone there and now.

But then Chi unpinned Cord from her gaze. "Anyway," she said to Connaught, "they left him where he fell, by a burned-out shack, a while before I came by from the looks of him. If anyone else was there first, they didn't get involved."

"There is little traffic through here," Connaught said. "A stage each month or so. We get few strangers."

"Seeing how you treat them," Cord said, "I'm not surprised."

"Give Bliss Basin a pass this season," Carlisle said. "The word is out."

"Guess that boy out back of the doctor's didn't hear," Cord snapped. "I suppose that's just what happens in these parts. People turn up dead and charred, so you put 'em somewhere out of the sun and go on about your business."

Fiona Cobb stared whitely at Cord. "You must understand—"

"*You* understand," Cord interrupted. "A man was murdered by a mob of cowards. That has got my goat—you figure out why. I know who was behind it, and I'm going to do something about it." He looked around at them. "Someone tell me I can't."

"We see how it is," Carlisle began.

"Not you," Cord said. "Not in a million years."

"There has been a serious rustling problem in this basin," Fiona Cobb said.

"You people got rustlers on the brain," Cord said. "You are seeing rustlers behind every tree."

"The point is that we are with you." Carlisle tried again. "That's what we want to talk to you about."

"Not yet," Cord said firmly. He put down his coffee cup. Chi's expression had unclouded. "Let's see to Wee Bill," Cord said to her. He had been out of action for a few days, but now he was back in business. He stood.

Chi nodded. "Good idea."

"I'll come along." Connaught rose. "That boy deserves some Christian rites, commending him to God's arms."

Cord was taken by surprise. "I can't see where it will do him any harm," Cord said. "At least not now."

Chapter Five

CORD STRAIGHTENED UP TO STRETCH THE muscles of his back and catch his breath. From this little grassy hump in the prairie, now eternal home to Wee Bill's clay-mound grave, Cord could see a good part of the basin. Off to the south a half mile or so down the gentle slope, the windmill rose to mark the town of Enterprise. The other way, maybe ten miles north, a dark blot on the sea of grass, was the windbreak closing in the headquarters of Bliss Ranch. As far again past the big house, at the foot of the mountains at the bowl's northwest rim, a line of trees marked the course of the little river that drained down from the high country and out through the North Gap, the other gateway of the otherwise-intact bowl. Cord wiped his forehead on the back of his shirt-sleeve. The day was ascending steadily toward real heat, despite the denial of the old snow on the north face slopes.

Cord bent to his work again, grooming the mound over the hole that held the corpse of Wee Bill Blewin, shaping the dense soil symmetrically and precisely and trying not to think about how many other men he had buried. The breeze from the west had stiffened, dry and hot; this was a wind for late July, Cord thought, not springtime. Connaught's horse looked up from where it was grazing nearby and snorted. The three of them had come out here on foot to do their burying, the body in its blanket slung over Connaught's saddle.

Cord stepped back, examined his work critically, and was satisfied. "If you've got to say something over him," he said, "now is the time."

F. X. Connaught stood by the grave with head bowed for a long moment of silence, then began to recite biblical verses having to do with death. Cord hunkered on his haunches off to the side and smoked, feeling less than comfortable with this. Formal religion had made him uncomfortable since his Lutheran youth, and funerals struck him as morbid brooding that came too late.

Connaught replaced his hat on his head finally and went out to his horse. "I bear this message," he said, picking up the bridle reins. "Mister Bliss wishes to see you."

"He is going to see me all right," Cord said. "We have got things to work out."

Connaught turned to mount up.

"*Alto*," Chi said. Connaught turned. "Are you a part of what goes on in this basin?"

Connaught regarded her. "In my way," he said. He looked off toward the ranch headquarters. "I have been with him near twenty years," he said. "When we met up, he was gathering west Texas range stock no one else wanted. Rib-scrawny cows on the hoof weren't worth two dollars, and we lived in dugouts and soddies and never ate nor drank anything that wasn't two parts dust."

Connaught looked back to Cord and Chi. "Mallory Bliss persevered, and then he prospered, as the Book promises a man will. Seven years ago this spring, with Texas closing in on him and his cattle, he started north. Late in the summer, when the first snows had already fallen in the mountains, he came into this place when there was, in that day, nothing but a garden of grass and that windmill, like to beckoning him in to make this country his own.

"Well, he did," Connaught said, "and now he is afraid others will try to seize it. He will do most anything to keep what is his."

"Including lynching," Cord said.

"'Judge not, that ye be not judged,'" Connaught quoted. "You cannot begrudge the man his ambition."

"Yeah," Cord said, "but there are other things I personally hold against your Mallory Bliss."

"He is not a bad man."

"People keep telling me that," Cord said. "Why is it I have so much trouble buying into the idea?"

Connaught seemed to think about that for a moment, as if the question were not rhetorical. "I will tell him to expect you."

"You do that," Cord said.

Cord shouldered his shovel and wiped his face again, watching Connaught ride off north toward the ranch. Chi appeared beside him. *Get it over with*, he thought. *Remind me of that old business if you got to, but get it done*.

But it turned out that her concern was not the past after all. "What now?"

"What do you figure?"

"Forgive and forget, maybe." But then she had to put in the needle. "Ride on to our sweet Bitter Root ranch."

"You are still feeling some edgy."

"I guess I just wonder," Chi said. "You never know. We might get out there sitting in one place and not like what we find. We might not even like each other."

The notion shook Cord, but he could see what she was talking about. "Homebodies," he said, smiling a little.

"We could turn out to be people we don't even know. Maybe it's too late for change, you some farmer and me some farmer's woman—that's a big bite to swallow whole." Chi looked at him ruefully, like she was sorry but couldn't explain it better.

"What do you want?" Cord demanded. "You want to die with your boots on, like in the dime books?"

"Maybe that is the only way," she said.

"Oh, hell," Cord said. "We both know better than that stuff. We've seen plenty of dying with your boots on. Nothing good about it." Cord turned into the hot wind. "Pretty soon the idea of gunfighters is going to be a bad joke. There'll be no place left for people like me and you."

"All right, then," Chi said. "If we are going to change, might as well do it all at once. Quit it cold."

Cord touched at the rope burn around his neck. "The thing is, I'd get to seeing this mark, and after a time I'd start waking up in the middle of the night from dreams of being hanged. Unless I get it fixed right now."

"Well, Mister Cord," Chi smiled slyly, "maybe you are not so ready to change as you think."

"Soon as this is over..."

"Certainly," Chi said solemnly. *"Por supuesto."*

Cord took a last drag on his smoke, spit into his palm, and put it out there. These handmade cigarettes would generally go out when dropped, but there was no sense in taking chances, not in this odd intemperate spring heat. "Let's get it done with," Cord said. The hot wind poured down toward the enisled town, swirling the blades of the tall windmill into a gray blur.

The café was empty, the table cleared, and the door locked, but the Enterprise Saloon was open for business now, if there were any business to be had in this basin. Cord followed Chi through the bat wings into its dimness.

The barroom, like the café, was neat and plain and mainly unpopulated. The tables were bare-topped but mostly free of scratches and cigarette burns, new as everything else man-made in these parts. Carlisle presided here as he had in the café that morning, stationed behind one end of the simple bar that ran along the back wall of the room, facing his only customer, Doctor Fiona Cobb.

The two of them were bent over coffee cups, heads down and close together. A whiskey bottle, about two-thirds full, sat between them and just to the side; it occurred to Cord that were this business to come to a fighting head, the doctor and the librarian would not be much use. But then he remembered he was not sure which side they were on anyway.

"Come on in," Carlisle said. "Take a drink on the management." Fiona Cobb did not look around at them.

"Where is everyone?" Chi said.

"They just left," Carlisle rejoined. But Cord's attention was on the other end of the bar. A five-gallon jug of heavy clear glass stood there, the sort in which vitriol was sometimes stocked. Its wide mouth was stoppered with a cork in which airholes had been bored, and something was moving inside. Cord bent to see better, squinting through the glass's distortion, his nose a couple of inches away.

The thing inside uncoiled itself, and Cord realized he was looking at a live rattlesnake—a split second before it struck at him. Cord yelped, "Holy Jesus!" and jerked away as the snake's twin fangs pinged against the inside of the thick glass. The back of Cord's legs hit a chair and he sat down heavily, almost toppled over. "What the hell?" he bleated. His heart was thumping. He hated snakes.

Carlisle was laughing. "It amuses the customers."

"Not this one." Cord got shakily to his feet. Chi was watching him with a serious, sympathetic face except for her eyes, which were laughing gaily. "We playing tricks or talking business?" Cord asked gruffly.

"We heard tricks *are* your business," Carlisle said.

"I'll show you a trick or two," Cord warned, "if you don't start getting down to cases. You were going to tell me about a job."

"But first tell us about the money you'll pay," Chi cut in. "That is the way we work."

Cord came down the bar, looking over his shoulder at the snake and feeling foolish.

"You will find us generous," Fiona Cobb said.

"Try to put a dollar figure to it," Chi said. "It's the only way you can compare offers."

Fiona Cobb looked puzzled. "I beg your pardon?"

"Soon as you've said your piece, I'll bet we will go out and ask your Mallory Bliss what he wishes to bid."

Cord shot her a look. She had figured something out that he had not yet come to.

Chi leered at the doctor. "You'd better come up with your best offer right off the bat."

Fiona Cobb looked genuinely surprised. "My interests and those of Mallory Bliss are identical."

"More or less," Carlisle put in.

"You offered a drink, Richard," Fiona Cobb snapped. "Fetch it." Carlisle straightened as if she had raised a hand to him. "We are partners," Fiona Cobb went on, turning back to Cord. "Mallory and I. He rules the range, but the town is mine."

"Your own town," Chi said. "Nice." Carlisle placed shot glasses in front of her and Cord, and snaked the bottle over in front of them. Cord put his hand palm-down over his glass. There would be no drinking for him until a bunch of items were settled.

"I was here first," Fiona Cobb said. "I have my rights."

"Time for a tale," Cord muttered under his breath.

"She fixed you up," Chi reminded him. "Be polite."

"I learned surgery from my father," Fiona Cobb said. "In New Haven, where I was raised. He was a professor at the medical college at Yale, and Cobb was one of his students. He was a good man," Fiona Cobb said, "but a poor doctor. A woman died in surgery and my husband was charged with murder."

"So you lit out for the territories." Carlisle offered the bottle.

Fiona Cobb nodded and watched him top off her coffee. "Our money ran out along the road here. That was eight years ago, in the springtime, and no one in this country except Blackfeet, Crow, a few wolfers, and one or two trappers who could not give it up. Settlers had passed it by for waterless, except for that bit of a river up north and that tiny creek you passed coming in. But we found a little cold spring that trickled out enough for the two of us. We thought we would fatten our stock on the free grass for a season, sell it out, and move on to San Francisco. Perhaps after a time my husband could safely practice medicine again."

"Things change," Chi said, glancing at Cord. But he was impatient and only half listening.

"Yes, they do," Fiona Cobb agreed. "My husband, for example, changed into a drunk. My luck was that he drilled this deep well and built that windmill and\tank before he died."

Cord perked up. "Of what?"

"Gambling and bad timing. My husband went up to Fort Benton to spread the word of sweet water in the basin. First, though, he needed a drink, and in a riverfront saloon he got into an arm-wrestling tussle with a pilot. My husband bet fifty cents on himself and broke the pilot's wrist." Fiona Cobb looked into her cup and dropped her voice. "He was a powerful man despite his disgrace. Well," she went on more briskly, "he knew anatomy and leverage, and he broke the man's wrist and laughed. The pilot took three quick drinks for his pain, then went out and came back with a gun. The pilot had to shoot left-handed, so he stood close and fired off all six rounds."

"*Lo siento*," Chi said politely. Fiona Cobb had been civil to her so far.

Fiona Cobb nodded her acknowledgment. "A week after I buried my husband, Mallory Bliss, with his foreman, our Mister F. X. Connaught, drove their Texas range stock into the basin and set up in a soddy." She drained her cup. "As the years followed, we prospered, jointly and severally."

"And into this Eden," Carlisle picked up, "came I."

"The snake?" Chi asked.

"Oh no," Carlisle told her. "The snake is in that jar over there."

"Make it short," Cord said to Carlisle.

"It all pertains," Carlisle insisted. "I arrived last summer. By then, Bliss was established and this town half-built."

"Why would someone like you come here?" Chi asked.

"Why not?"

"He was kicked off the monthly stagecoach," Fiona Cobb said. "For cheating a whiskey drummer out of thirty dollars in a game of cribbage."

Carlisle examined his nails. "He would never have caught me," he said, "if I hadn't been drunk. The funny thing is that I don't usually cheat." He smiled at Chi. "Anyway, not at cards. That drummer had cheated first."

"Is that the way you remember it, Richard?" Fiona Cobb asked.

"Sometimes," Carlisle said serenely. "I landed at Doctor Cobb's feet and was taken in like a lost lamb. The gods do conspire."

"Really interesting," Cord said, "your life stories and all. I could go on listening all the day long, but I've got another appointment later on." Cord placed both hands flat on the bar and leaned a little toward Carlisle. "Now tell me what I want to know: How did that windmill in the prairie turn into this spanking new empty town? Who made you the saloonkeep—nobody would trust their whiskey to you."

"Temporary post," Carlisle said. "Like I told you, I'm a librarian."

"And I am Prince Albert." Cord turned his stare on Fiona Cobb. "What about you, Miss Doctor. How is the healing business hereabouts?"

"More to the point," Chi said, "whom do you wish killed?"

"Take it easy," Carlisle said.

"I have been." Cord spun on his heel. "But now I am getting worked up," he warned.

"Good time for it," Chi said calmly.

Cord didn't get what she meant for a moment, but then he heard the horses too. A moment after that, they came into view, four mounted men. The frame of the saloon's front window cut off their heads, but Cord could see plenty enough: in one set of stirrups, blocky square-toed steel-lined fighting boots; above another saddle, the empty right sleeve of a flannel shirt pinned to the shoulder.

Cord edged back against the bar, where he could cover the sweep of the room. "Trouble, maybe," he said, watching the door.

"No maybe," Chi said. "I am going to make some trouble for sure."

Cord was startled at her vehemence. She looked at him and smiled bitterly. "Don't you understand how badly I hate what they did to you?"

Cord was pleased to hear that, but by then bootheels were clattering up on the boardwalk and there were new matters on which to concentrate. The one in the fighting boots led them in, and right away Cord was certain that despite the hoods the night riders had worn, this was not the man who had been so hot to see him swing, over Bliss's argument. This man was too slim and narrow-shouldered, and he carried himself all wrong: He was about twenty and twitchy, as if, unable to wait for an excuse for trouble, he might manufacture his own.

If Chi didn't beat him to it. Cord heard her angry derisive snort at this boy and recognized her impatience as the sort that often led to bad times for whoever was annoying her. These men were night riders for certain: There would not be two men in this basin with only a left arm, and the kid's boots were no coincidence.

The kid and the one-armed man came into the barroom. The other two slipped in behind and took up positions flanking the door, watching Cord and Chi with aggressive curiosity. One was a barrel-chested flat-nosed jasper in a derby hat, the other a thin light-skinned Negro with wavy, hennaed hair.

The kid moved up to the bar, slapped his palm on its top, and gave Chi a lickerish leer. Cord ignored him and said to the one-armed man, "I bet they call you Lefty."

"They always try to," the one-armed man said. "But Pincus is my name, and I make them use it."

"A one-armed man can't hide under a hood," Cord said. "You ought to wear a flour sack, right down to your knees."

"It'd be hard to shoot," Pincus said.

Cord smiled pleasantly. "How would it be," he inquired pleasantly, "if I tore your other goddamned arm out of the socket right now, you night-riding son of a bitch? How hard would it be to shoot then?"

"Hard for me," Pincus said flatly. "For Magee and Sheeny over there"—he nodded over his shoulder at the man in the derby and the Negro, both of whom now stood with hands on gun butts—"not so hard probably."

"Yeah, it would." Chi's right hand was under her serape. "Hard as hell with holes in their guts."

Carlisle broke from where he stood and came down the bar. "What do you want?" he said to the kid, not nicely. Fiona Cobb had not moved. Cord wondered if she were drunk, or braver than he'd thought.

"A bottle of the good stuff," the kid snapped. He pulled a gold coin from his vest pocket, held it on edge, and set it spinning with a flick of his forefinger. Carlisle snatched up the coin, set out a glass, and filled it from a bottle with a gold label.

"You gonna shoot me for taking a drink, dark lady?" The Negro gave Chi a too-bright look as he ambled toward the bar.

"Come ahead and see," Chi said.

The Negro looked uncertain. He spotted the big jar and veered that way, pretending to look it over with interest. But then he spotted the rattlesnake and stopped pretending. "The hell is this supposed to be for?"

The kid drank his drink and grinned over at the Negro. "You ain't been in here before, Sheeny." The kid slid down the bar. "I'm gonna show you a trick."

"I got a trick for you, *pendejo*," Chi said.

"I'll get to you by and by, lady," the kid said, not looking at her. He had no idea how close to the edge she already was, Cord saw. Pincus stepped back to watch the goings-on from one side, and Magee looked alert from his position by the door.

"I bet twenty bucks," the kid announced, "that you can't keep your hand flat on the bottle glass when the snake strikes at it."

"Say what?" Sheeny said.

"Human nature. You'll jerk back like you was really bit."

"Likely I would," Sheeny said. "Except I ain't playing."

"You figure he is gonna come right through that glass?" the kid taunted. "You think that is some kind of ghost snake from one of your mammy's fairy stories?"

"Easy now, Short String," Sheeny said in a soft, careful voice.

The kid went rigid. "What was that name again?"

"Luke," Sheeny said sullenly. "The name is Luke."

Luke produced a twenty dollar gold piece. That would be most of a month's salary for a cowhand in these parts, Cord guessed, but then these boys were not cowhands. "Play my game, Sheeny," Luke smirked, shooting a prideful glance at Chi, as if assuming she had to be impressed by his manly behavior.

"I do not like this boy's manner," Chi said clearly.

"It's his boots that get my goat," Cord said.

The kid whirled. "Too bad," he said. "Too bad what you don't like." Cord wondered again how fast he would be with his left hand, if it came to that.

"Okay, Luke," Sheeny said quickly. "If the only thing'll make you happy is to see a nigger jump, I'll go along. But I ain't paying you a double sawbuck for the privilege."

Luke stared at Cord, as if gazes were gunfights. "Drink," he snapped, and looked away. Carlisle refilled his glass and the kid poured it down.

"Here is a *muchacho* who needs a lesson on what makes a man," Chi said.

At the door, Magee looked less sure of himself. "Look, here goes," Sheeny said quickly. *Get the boy out of here*, Cord almost said. But he saw the way Chi was looking and checked himself. She had something in mind—though he was not sure exactly what it was and thought he would not like it so much if he did.

Sheeny placed his hand on the glass. The snake lay in an oblivious coil. Sheeny tapped a fingernail on the other side of the bottle, and the snake stirred. A bit of sweat shined on Sheeny's brown-yellow forehead. Cord watched, fascinated despite himself.

The snake lifted its head and pivoted the upper half of its three-foot body. Its rattle began to chatter, the sound deadened by the bottle's cork stopper. Sheeny worked the tip of his tongue over his lower lip.

The snake struck, its triangular head bouncing off the glass. Sheeny jerked back his hand and barked, "Damn!"

"He get you, Sheeny?" Luke laughed. "You need some-one to cut you and suck the poison?"

"Muchacho!"

Luke turned slowly away from the Negro, putting on his dirty smirk. "Hold your water, lady."

"Now we will play," Chi said. "You and me."

Luke looked pleased. This woman had picked him out of the crowd. "You want to hold onto a snake," Luke said, "I got one you'll like."

"You are a filthy little boy," Chi said. "I am going to teach you a lesson in manners."

Pincus snickered. Luke shot him a furious look.

"I am ready," Chi said. "Bet me two hundred dollars I can't keep my hand on the jar."

She was pushing all the way now: Trouble was here.

"Maybe you don't have two hundred dollars," Chi said.

"I got it," Luke said in a husky voice. He took out a pocketbook and currency, showed it to her. He removed bills, fanned them out like a poker hand, then squared them and stuffed them in his shirt pocket. "Let's see yours."

Chi smiled maliciously. "No."

Fiona Cobb looked up for the first time. Her expression was almost clinically curious as she examined Chi, as if she had just discovered a new subspecies among human females. Well, she sure as hell was that, Cord thought.

Luke's expression turned tentative. He was starting to get the idea that the water was rising and wondering how deep it was going to get. Over his head, maybe.

Chi stared at him and placed her hand on the jar.

The snake struck.

Chi did not move a muscle.

"You got to watch him!" Luke bleated, like a kid in a school yard.

"Okay." Chi smiled at Cord. "If the *chiquito* moves, kill him."

"My pleasure."

"I got my boys with me!" Luke whined.

"Do shut up, sonny," Carlisle said. Even the bartender was pushing Luke around now.

Chi put her hand on the glass again and slowly lowered her head to watch the snake. She stared at it while it struck a second time, a third, a fourth, its rattle chattering madly. Chi slowly removed her hand. "*Probrecito*," she said to the snake. "You will break your fangs."

She smiled prettily at Luke. "Give me my money, *cabrónito*."

"You go to hell." Luke turned away. "Let's get out of here." Sheeny and Pincus were ahead of him as they went toward the door.

"You forgot your whiskey," Chi said softly. "Didn't you want to take the bottle?"

Luke looked from the liquor on the bar to the other three men waiting by the door, Magee and Sheeny and Pincus. He licked his lips, knew where he was now but too late to do anything about it. Chi had him buffaloed—and yet only the yellowest of dogs would allow himself to be hazed out of there this way.

Hazed out by a woman.

Luke turned, took two steps back toward the bar. As he reached out, the bottle exploded.

Chi's hand was clear of the serape now, and her Colt was in it. She turned the gun on the three bunched near the door.

"You tried to hang my partner," she said.

"We didn't, though," Pincus said gently.

"You are dog-assed mobsters, afraid to even show your faces. Deny it."

"We are members of the Bliss Basin Vigilance Committee," Pincus said, "maintaining order in absence of established law." Magee edged a step away to one side.

Carlisle reached back and set another bottle on the bar. Chi's back was to him.

Luke reached for the second bottle, and Chi fired across her body and blew it to pieces. She had barely looked to aim; she was doing magic today.

She said, watching the men at the door, "Give me my money, or I will take it off your corpse." She let Luke have a quick look at her expression. "You bet more than you could afford, and you lost. Now you've got to pay up."

Cord saw that there would be a fight. No stopping it now: One on one against the kid, but it would be like killing him in cold blood. She was faster, no question in the world.

Still, Cord liked it not at all. It wasn't one on one, and when the indiscriminate shooting started in this place, no telling who would get hit. Well, it looked too late to stop it now. Besides, she must have a reason for doing this deadly thing, and she was his partner. Cord would back her play no matter what.

Fiona Cobb moved around behind the end of the bar then, where there was cover behind which to duck, though she did not look frightened but rather anticipatory, a bit flushed. Carlisle stayed where he was, both hands in sight.

"You got your choice," Chi told the kid.

Luke was thinking hard and coming up empty. Without taking his eyes from Chi, he said to Cord, "You let your woman fight your battles for you?"

"You made the bet, boy." Cord laughed; best to keep the edge on the other side. "She always shoots for a man's right eye. Ask me why."

Luke was in alien territory. "Why?" he rasped.

"It disturbs his aim."

Chi laughed.

Luke blanched. "Listen up," he said. But it was too late for this Short String: The first gun went off.

The shot, very loud in the room, came from the rifle that had suddenly appeared in Carlisle's hands. It cracked through the wood of the door between the gunmen there, Magee on one side, Pincus and Sheeny on the other.

Magee was frozen with his revolver barrel nearly clear of his holster, facing Chi's Colt.

"What now, little man?" Chi swept aside her serape to expose her holster, dropped her Colt into it. "Now you are way ahead of me. Maybe here is your lucky chance."

Magee hesitated a long beat—and went for it, tried to draw on her. She beat him by a lot and put a clean shot right through his pump. Blood splattered the wall behind him.

Chi watched Magee's body ooze down the wall. "Maybe not," she said.

It could have ended there—should have, if the boy had sense. But then the moment was gone, and he was proving he had none at all, pulling his gun and giving out a hard grunt. Cord beat him left-handed and shot him from the side. Luke screamed and spun away and went down.

"That's enough," Carlisle ordered. He was covering Sheeny and Pincus with his rifle. They kept their hands carefully clear of their weapons.

"Doesn't have to be over yet," Chi spat at Sheeny and Pincus. "We can have lots more fun at your expense." She looked mad enough to chew nails.

"It is, though," Pincus said quickly. "Over and done."

"Not quite." Chi went up to Pincus, her gun on him all the while. "There is one more piece of old business. Who leads the night riders? Who was so itchy to kill my partner?"

"Mallory Bliss," Pincus said. "Everybody knows that."

Chi placed her gun muzzle against his one elbow.

"A man called Stringer," Pincus said.

"Big wide man?" Cord asked. "Rides a black horse with three white stockings, and wears fighting boots like that boy?"

"That's him."

"You tell him that we have got some things to settle," Cord said.

Pincus glanced at Luke's bleeding body. "You've got that right, pal," Pincus said. "You just killed his kid brother."

But Cord had already guessed that part. "Take your trash and give us some peace."

"I got a feeling you are going to see us again," Pincus said malevolently.

"Better bring an army," Cord snapped. He never felt good after a fight. "Now do what I say."

Pincus and Sheeny came forward, got the corpses under the arms, and started to drag them out.

"Hold it," Chi said. She bent and pulled the two hundred dollars from Luke's shirt pocket, watching the two men, challenging someone to object. "Now it is all right," she said.

Everything hung silently while Pincus and Sheeny drug their drinking cronies out the door. Cord watched through the window as they loaded the bodies over their saddles and tied them on.

Chi turned away from the door, her expression composed. Cord was annoyed. He'd already told her clearly that he meant to do something about the men who tried to hang him, but here she had nearly taken the play away from him. Instead of deliberation, she had acted with something near to craziness.

"Well, now." She put her gun away under her serape, gazing back at him. "Maybe one more drink for the road."

Cord stared at her. The oddest hunch crossed his mind: For some reason unexpressed but likely having to do with whatever was eating at her, had she chosen to challenge their mortality? Cord felt hot: Where was her right to draw him into her quick mad life-and-death games?

"All right?" she said lightly, and moved past. Well, it had turned out all right, that he must admit. Then he realized the rest of it. She had turned away from the boy Luke, put her back to him and left her protection to Cord's weak left hand, because she *knew*: as always, one-handed or no, Cord would be ready, and able, to cover her. The old instincts and cues of partnership remained intact. What happened in Livingston was behind them.

She was correct after all: they still worked together pretty damned effectively. What else did she know, Cord wondered. . . .

He jammed his Colt back into the holster and turned back to the bar. Carlisle let the hammer down on the rifle. "For a librarian," Cord said, "you are pretty damned fast with a long gun."

Carlisle lay the weapon on the bar and looked as if he would say something. Instead, he merely shook his head. His face was a little paste-colored.

"If you have any other colorful secrets," Chi said, "now is the time to lay them out."

"You gonna shoot me in the elbow if I don't talk?" Carlisle snapped. But his voice sounded reedy, and all of a sudden he crossed his arms and lay his head down on the bar top.

"Richard!" Fiona Cobb said with concern. She filled a shot glass with whiskey and pressed it into Carlisle's hand.

He raised his head and sucked it down. Fiona Cobb poured a refill.

Carlisle straightened, holding the glass. "We are done," he said in a voice thick with despair. He gestured with the glass. "To happier trails," he said miserably, and drank the whiskey.

"It could be okay, Richard," Fiona Cobb said urgently. "We still have them." She waved in Chi's direction without looking toward her.

"I don't like being talked about that way," Chi said. "Like I'm not here."

"You're right," Fiona Cobb said quickly. "I am sorry."

"That's better." But Chi looked a bit surprised at the apology from this lady.

"Run out if you must, Richard," Fiona Cobb said. "It won't be the first time."

"For either of us." Carlisle reached for the bottle.

Fiona Cobb snatched it back away from him. Carlisle blinked. The doctor set the bottle on the back bar. "To now we were not involved in any way with Stringer's mob." She turned to face the three of them. "Mallory is responsible for them."

"No blood on your hands," Cord said.

"Two of his men died in our place," Fiona Cobb said. "We've taken a side—at least Stringer will see it that way. You don't know him."

"Maybe we do," Chi said.

Fiona Cobb was not paying attention. "You are right, Richard. We must decide now whether to stay or go." She looked up at Cord and Chi. "And so must you."

"But bear this in mind," Carlisle warned. "If you stay, you are in on the trouble. You got no choice at all."

"I can't stand being told to fight or run," Chi said.

"Not that it hasn't happened before," Cord muttered.

"Well, if I've got to hear it," Chi said, "I better be told the whys and wherefores. I want to know every damned thing."

"Before we make any rash decisions." Cord was still thinking about the late gunfight.

"Time for true talk," Chi said.

"Yes," Fiona Cobb said, as if that had not occurred to her. "Of course."

Chapter Six

IN MOST OF THE TOWNS THROUGH WHICH
Cord's wanderings had taken him over the years, a few
books were set aside somewhere. Especially here on the
northern plains, where winters were hard and dark and short
on entertainment and escape, books were dear and shared.
In the corner of a saloon or mercantile, perhaps in the county
sheriff's office, folks set up a lending library of a few dozen
volumes of books for rent or to swap.

And Cord had seen true libraries as well, massive stone
temples in San Francisco and Los Angeles and Denver. He
knew there existed a wealth of words published between
hard boards. But he would never have expected to find such
a library here in the middle of 750 square miles of nothing
but grass and cows.

The Enterprise Free Library had been constructed and
stocked with care and bibliophilic devotion. Big glass win-

dows let in the midmorning sun to the three reading tables with matched chairs lined up along a wide middle aisle. To either side shelves rose toward the ceiling, filled with books whose spines and edges were free of dust. An oak countertop desk faced the double front doors. Behind it were shelved Webster's *Dictionary of the American Language* and other dictionaries, in French and Spanish, an *Encyclopaedia Britannica*; biographical collections, including Samuel Johnson's *Lives of the Poets* and Thomas North's translation of Plutarch, *Lives of the Noble Grecians and Romans*; a King James Bible; and the works of Shakespeare.

Cord stood paging at an atlas of the world, thinking this library would be no more unlikely if discovered in the heart of farthest Africa. It was an eerie place, carefully provisioned with everything but readers. It must have been an expensive and epic undertaking, freighting all these books up the Missouri or on the railroad, and then by wagon across the prairie, protecting the cargo from rain and dust. Cord closed the atlas and turned to Fiona Cobb and Richard Carlisle.

"Why?"

"Bliss likes to read," Carlisle said, as if that explained everything.

"Speak up." Chi came out of the shadows of a high shelf.

"Culture, knowledge, and high thought." Carlisle spread his arms, palms up. "The common bedrock of order. And order," Carlisle said, "is the one true ambition of Mallory Bliss."

Carlisle ran a thumbnail along the cloth spines of a shelf of books. He turned, pinned in a shaft of sunbeam streaming down from one of the high windows. "Behold his beacon," Carlisle said. "The shining light that will bring society to this wilderness."

"What are you talking about?" Cord still felt irritable.

"It will not always be this way," Fiona Cobb said.

"I hope to hell not," Cord said, misunderstanding.

"Enterprise will be a true community some day. People will stream to this place and establish themselves."

"Is that what you want?" Chi said.

"It's what he wants," Carlisle said with some awe, as if the pronoun referenced the Lord himself.

Fiona Cobb leaned back against the oak countertop and regarded them. "When Mallory came here, the country was empty, and his alone. That changed within a few years. The railroad drove past Miles City. Homesteaders were settling not too far away."

"He was losing his grip," Carlisle said.

Fiona Cobb related the story in a soft voice, and truth to tell, the library did provoke reverence. On the one hand, Bliss hated the idea of people claiming homestead right to even the smallest piece of "his" land. This basin, this great thirty-mile bowl of grass, demarked by the mountains rising on every side—it was his. He was here first, and he worked this land and made it productive, and no one would take it from him. On the other hand, to live as a gentleman, he must live among others. There was no civilization without society.

"So Mallory determined to mold a society to his own specifications," Fiona Cobb said. "A benevolent fiefdom, his empire—in his image, by his whim. Finally, a couple of years ago, he was wealthy enough to go to work. The first step was to invent this town of Enterprise."

"The petty bourgeoisie," Carlisle said.

"Talk English," Chi said.

"The merchant class," Carlisle explained. "They would be his subjects. Around his market town, people would take up small parcels of land on which to live and work. He would even allow them to raise produce and chickens and hogs for themselves. The open range would be his alone."

"Cockamamie plan," Chi said.

"Someone should have told him," Carlisle said mildly. "Too late now."

But Cord was thinking that it all made an odd sort of sense, as much sense as this library anyway. He was starting to put the pieces together. "Your windmill," he said to Fiona Cobb. "Your windmill and your water."

Fiona Cobb nodded. "That dictated his townsite, of course. The water for his ranchstead is diverted from the river, and by late summer there is barely enough for his people and stock. I gave him his townsite."

"And he gave you his town," Chi said.

"The hotel, saloon, café, and mercantile," she confirmed. "In exchange for rights to my water."

"And a lady doctor thrown into the bargain," Cord said.

"He had plenty of time to get used to the idea of a woman ministering to the ill. His third winter here, Mallory was gun shot in a hunting accident. I took out the bullet."

"You never told me that," Carlisle said. He shook his head. "Circles within circles."

"He set me up in my surgery to serve the people when they come. In the meanwhile I patch up cowhands when necessary and see to his veterinary needs."

"And one day last summer," Chi said, "the stage driver tossed you a bartender."

"I am a man of parts," Carlisle said. "Some fair skill at bartending and cooking have carried me through sparse times. And I was a surveyor once, so when I arrived I got construction work until I'd ingratiated myself. Then, when Bliss learned I was a librarian and a schoolteacher to boot—"

"A schoolteacher?" Chi echoed.

Carlisle nodded happily. "I sold myself to Bliss as a graduate of Oberlin College of Ohio."

"Are you?"

"Not exactly. I was a student there for six months, but there was some trouble with a professor's daughter."

"Picking on little girls," Chi sneered.

"But I was a little boy," Carlisle said coyly.

"Sometimes, Richard," Fiona Cobb said, "you act as if you still are."

Carlisle colored. "Be that as it may," he went on quickly, "Bliss's plan for attracting people of refinement included a schoolhouse, and there I was."

Cord watched dust specks turn lazily in the sunlight. It was warm in the close building. "So far, Bliss has done a fine job putting together his dream town," he observed. "He's got a doctor whose patients are mostly horses and cows, a schoolteacher without pupils, a mercantile and hotel without customers, and our Mr. Carlisle here, scholar and rifleman."

"There is one other thing he has got," Chi pointed out. "Serious gun trouble, right around the corner." She stood facing Fiona Cobb, arms akimbo. "Now you tell us: What is wrong with your man? How does he square his great plans with hanging strangers?"

Chi's bluntness caught Fiona Cobb off-guard. "You can understand," she said reasonably.

"Not ever," Chi said evenly.

"Mallory is not well."

"Mister Mallory Bliss," Carlisle said, "is our Ahab, and order is his white whale. The trouble is, the old boy is nutty as Melville's captain."

"Well now," Cord said with some exasperation. "That explains it all."

Fiona Cobb turned abruptly. In the shadow of the bookshelf she ran her forefinger over spines, extracted a thick volume bound in black cloth. She handed it to Chi, and Cord read the title over her shoulder: *Elements of Physiological Psychology*, by George Trumbull Ladd.

"What the hell?" Cord was perplexed.

Chi tapped her temple with a forefinger. "Serious sorts of craziness."

"I believe Mallory suffers from megalomania," Fiona Cobb said. "A delusional mental disorder marked by feelings of personal omnipotence."

"What in God's name does that mean?" Cord asked.

"Mallory cannot distinguish right from wrong anymore," Fiona Cobb said.

"Well, then everything is okay," Cord said with heavy sarcasm. "Now that I know he is daft, I feel a lot better about him trying to stretch me."

"He cannot stop himself," Fiona Cobb said simply. "And he was misled."

"I'll tell the world," Cord snapped. "Your man is living in his bad dreams."

"Not entirely," Carlisle said. "The rustler problem is real enough."

"Too bad."

Carlisle pursed his lips. "Ranchers all over this territory have been losing up to ten percent of their stock. Not the culls either, but fat cows right down the line. And in this big basin, with no law and few hands per the acre, Bliss was suffering bad as anyone."

"A rich man," Chi said. "Why should we care for him?"

She looked at Cord. "He should have been a banker in our earlier days. We would have known how to do him then."

Cord had to laugh.

"A few months ago," Fiona Cobb said, "Mallory attended the annual meeting of the Stock Growers Association in Miles City. Rustling was on everyone's mind, and some of the big ranchers were clamoring for vigilante action. Mallory took the other side; were they to resort to lawlessness, it would be broadcast in the Eastern papers."

"And the proper citizens would never come to populate his empire," Chi said.

"Some of the ranchers sensed Mallory's true sentiments," Fiona Cobb went on. "They came to him privately and promised to back him—surreptitiously, of course. He agreed to run a sort of vigilante pilot project in the basin."

"But he was shrewd, our patriarch," Carlisle said. "He couldn't involve the cowhands that would stay on with him in later, more genteel years. He told his big cattlemen buddies that this was a job for professionals, men who knew what they were about. When it was done, they'd be paid off and sent on their way. No gunfighters wanted in our fine community," Carlisle said sardonically. "Not after they've outlived their usefulness." He looked from Cord to Chi. "Present company excepted, of course."

"This was all his idea?" Chi asked. "He didn't happen to ask your opinion before he brought a dozen hired killers into your home country?"

"Actually," Carlisle said, "he didn't. Believe it or don't."

"We learned of his plan two or three days before Stringer and his men rode in," Fiona Cobb said. "I was at the ranch for calving—I have little else to do around here—and Mallory told me the whole story. I think he may have been seeking my approval."

"And you gave it to him."

"I thought he was wrong and told him so," the doctor said with some heat. "I tried to persuade him to call his plan off."

"You should have tried harder."

"He was possessed. His zeal overcame his reason."

"Sure enough," Carlisle said. "Just a week ago, his night-riders killed an innocent man."

"How's that?" Cord was startled.

"Stringer and a couple of his riders came on a middle-aged geezer running four horses and two mules near the North Gap. They killed him for a rustler and took the animals. Bliss wasn't with them. Anyway, late the next day a fellow rode into town looking for his father. He was supposed to meet him here—Enterprise was just a spot on the map to him—and help drive the stock to the railhead. He had a bill of sale for the six animals."

"Kind of embarrassing for you," Cord said. "Having to tell him what had happened."

"We didn't know," Fiona Cobb said.

"Convenient."

"We told him his father had probably ridden by in the night," Carlisle said. "He didn't believe it, and neither did we. But he went on south anyway."

"I went to Mallory and demanded to know the truth," Fiona Cobb said. "Mallory knew by then; Stringer had bragged. Mallory told me the old man had no business drifting through his valley, not these days. But in his eyes I saw that knowledge was returning. . . . Maybe he was coming to understand after all. . . . "

"You make it sound like a mistake," Cord said. "Call it by its real name: murder. If Wee Bill Blewin was telling the truth—and I mean to find out someday—that's two murders, two innocent men killed dead."

"If you had known," Chi asked quietly, "would you have told that boy the truth about his father?" Cord regarded her: in the quiet light her olive face glowed like the Madonna's.

"What could it accomplish?" Fiona Cobb said.

"It would have shown backbone," Chi said, "and that maybe you weren't as crazy as Bliss."

Fiona Cobb's face fell. She suddenly looked to Cord as if she had gone too long since her last drink.

"You two are his collaborators," Cord said. "You deserve your troubles."

"You haven't heard all of them yet," Carlisle said mildly. "There is one more odd item. Since Stringer and his thugs have been in these precincts, Bliss's losses to rustling has gone *up*. Nearly a third of his calves seem to be getting lost lately. What do you make of that?"

"Maybe it is the two of you," Chi said.

"You know who it is."

"So Stringer has cut in for a hunk of Bliss's business. Don't expect us to feel sorry for him." Cord grinned. "I can see why it would make you nervous, though. You and Bliss have lost control."

"Stringer means to bleed this basin dry," Carlisle said.

"And that gunfight in the bar will force his hand," Fiona Cobb said. "He knows you—what sort of man you are. He will figure you have allied yourselves with us, so he will act immediately, before you have a chance to form a plan or recruit others."

"He's got some wrong ideas."

"But he doesn't know it. It's as I said: Like it or no, you must decide whether to fight or run."

"Well, now," Cord said. "We have come to the point at

last. You want us to stop Stringer for you. You want us to restore your emperor to his throne."

"Not exactly," Chi emended. "You want us to save his bacon—yours as well."

"Ten thousand dollars," Fiona Cobb said.

"Show me your money," Chi snapped.

Fiona Cobb colored. "He will pay. I guarantee he will." Chi glowered at her.

"Wait up a minute." Carlisle paused, looked from Chi to Cord, and when he went on, the irony and subtle toying tones were gone from his voice. "This woman here has had some tough breaks in her life."

Fiona Cobb looked at Carlisle and frowned but said nothing.

"Facts are facts, and we have laid them out for you honestly," Carlisle went on. "Bliss has gone wrong, and it's backfired on him. And if he loses, so does Fiona. Loses everything."

"And you," Chi said. "You have a stake as well."

"Sure," Carlisle agreed. "I like it here. But running is enough of a habit with me that I can do it one more time without it hurting too badly. Besides, I haven't invested much time or trouble in making a place for myself here." He glanced at the doctor. "It doesn't make so much difference either way for me."

"Richard," Fiona Cobb said in a soft voice.

"Forget me." Carlisle looked away with some difficulty. "But this lady here has already eaten her helpings of bad times. Now she has something, something she worked for, and by my lights she deserves a chance at keeping it. This basin could be her last good road to daylight."

"If Stringer is stopped," Cord said.

Fiona Cobb put her hand on Carlisle's arm near the elbow.

"I'm not a brave man," Carlisle said to Cord. "Don't depend on my work with that rifle in the bar. I can handle guns and think quickly; you got to do both in some of the lines I have pursued. But inside I am scared spitless, and because of that, I can't ever count on myself in a fight. That's why I tend toward running out."

"Then run out," Chi said.

Carlisle shook his head. "I guess I won't." He put his hand over Fiona Cobb's. "You back this woman, I'll side you best I can. That's my last best offer."

Afterward, you could almost always pin the moment when you were in all the way and no looking back. In earlier times it would have come the instant Cord came back to consciousness, after those bastards made the mistake of changing their minds about killing him. But now Cord realized that all the way to here, at least a part of him had toyed with the idea of giving up his vengeance, turning on this basin and riding out.

It wouldn't have worked anyway, Cord saw. He would have hated himself mightily for an endless time.

Cord cleared his throat to break the moment of awkward silence. He looked at Chi for a sign, but her face was blank and she was watching Carlisle and Fiona Cobb, standing hand in hand. "Say we agree to take care of Stringer's bunch," Cord said. "Who takes care of Bliss?"

"I can handle him," Fiona Cobb said.

"Can you handle us?" Chi asked.

Fiona Cobb gave her a perplexed look.

"You people started out with a few unorganized rustlers, stray gatherers who weren't much more than an annoyance. You traded them for a bunch of professional thugs who are about ready to take you over. Now you figure to trade them for us." Chi smiled wickedly. "We could be the worst yet."

Fiona Cobb was startled. "Should we worry about you?"

"Not unless you cross us up," Cord said briskly. *"Qué piensas?"* he said to Chi.

"I think," Chi said, "that we should accept Senor Bliss's invitation. I have never seen an empire before. Anyway," she went on, "we will have everyone's story in hand. Maybe then we can sort out the bullshit from the barley."

"I doubt it," Cord said, suddenly weary. "But let's try it out."

Chapter Seven

OFF TO THE EAST ON THE NEAR SLOPE OF A little fold in the contour of the basin floor, a herd of twenty or so cows and calves grazed at peace amid a flock of four or five dozen white-tailed prairie deer. The cattle Cord and Chi passed watched incuriously as the deer, almost dainty in their quick graceful movements, flitted among the stolid oblivious cattle. *The calf and the young lion and the fatling together*, Cord thought, remembering Isaiah. But where was the little child who would lead them. No one in this valley but mad old men . . .

The hot dry wind coming from the mountains off west was constant, mechanical, and a little alarming; here was the sort of wind that wicked water from the creeks and stock tanks, raised clouds of topsoil, and swept the sky clear of rain clouds, a wind that could send the flames of a careless campfire over the grass with the speed of an express train.

If this strange spring wind kept up through much of the summer, it could do a job of devastation that would put Stringer and his bunch to shame.

The wind had spun the blades of the tall windmill as Cord and Chi rode beneath it, and it continued to pluck at them as they headed north on the stage road. An hour further on, a wide track forked off northwest, toward the windbreak sheltering the headquarter of Bliss Ranch. Most of another hour of riding had brought them here to where they could make out individual structures behind the row of tall cottonwood.

Cord reined up and peered up that way, pretending to be taking a cautious look-see. Actually, there were things he wished to get off his mind before this business passed into its next stage. Chi's mood had improved since Livingston, but far as he was concerned, it still had a ways to go. "You pushed things pretty hard, back in that saloon," Cord said.

"Piss on it," Chi said. "Two less night riders to concern ourselves with. Isn't that what we are doing here?"

"Not entirely," Cord explained patiently. "We are doing what we have to."

"Which is?"

"I'm still working on figuring that out." But that was only partially true, and she knew it. He did not have to explain that this Stringer had to be killed, face-to-face in a fair fight, if possible, but killed for certain. Ten years on the outlaw trail had taught this much at least: This sort of conflict never healed itself but festered and putrefied. Stringer knew the rules as well—knew at least that there were men like Cord who lived by them—so Stringer would force the fight anyway, knowing it inevitable, preferring to take the advantage of his force. If he didn't simply attempt a bushwhack . . .

"The longer we ride, the more baggage we seem to pick up." Chi could have been reading his thoughts, and maybe she could. . . . "If there's any unfinished business in with it, figure on it jumping out to bite you every time you try to unpack."

"Well, sure," Cord said. "Once we get that place of ours, I don't want to be wondering every time there is a knock on the door if it is someone looking for trouble, someone we forgot to kill. Hell on the appetite."

Chi smiled tentatively. Cord had guessed lucky: it was the right tone to take with her right now.

"But this finishes it," Cord went on more firmly. "I am done with this nomad life. It is a long odds proposition, and I have already won my share. I am cashing in my checks."

"Some people are magnets for trouble," Chi said. "Maybe trouble is in your nature, and you will never get away from it no matter how far you ride."

Cord stared across at the ranch. "I could be killed today," Cord said. "I don't expect it to happen, but I hate the possibility. The fastest gun in the world—and I'm not him, even right-handed—is no match for a bullet in the back of the head."

"Hey, *querido*."

Cord looked at her.

"I won't let anybody shoot you in the back."

"I appreciate that," Cord said, "but it could be that you are somewhere out of range—like the other night when I almost got hanged."

Chi looked away, and Cord knew this was his chance. "I tell you now, Chi: When this is over, I am done." Cord drew a deep breath. "I am taking my share of what we got put away, and I am retiring. I want you to be with me, now and always, but I am done no matter what." *Done and buried alive if you leave me*, he thought, tried to say it, and could not quite get it out.

But she knew that, because she was regarding him with no outrage, her handsome dark eyes shaded by the wide brim of her sombrero. She said his name sweetly, and Cord waited for her to go on.

But then her eyes shifted and she was looking past him. Cord let out breath he had not realized he was holding and turned in his saddle.

A half mile or more off west across the prairie, a lone figure sat a dark horse. Cord could not make out the rider at that distance, but Chi could always outsee him, and when he turned back and saw her expression, Cord knew another joker had been dealt into this hand, from a deck from which plenty enough had already come.

It wasn't one of Stringer's men; they did not ride alone. Suddenly Cord got a hunch that bloomed into something like certainty. The missing character in this drama who was bound to show up—and what perfect goddamned timing. Chi said nothing, and the moment they had shared was broken. She thumped her mare and rode on. Cord followed, swearing to himself.

Up ahead a high arch of gnarled scrub logs woven together formed a gate over the road, with a shingle hanging from rawhide thongs proclaiming this Bliss Ranch. No one challenged them as they rode beneath it.

And into as fine a spread as Cord had ever seen, one that would make any stockman sick with yearning. It was an oasis, a sprawling patch of spring green, maybe two thousand acres of irrigated hayland. Long straight-arrow ditches ran in from the river to the north, filling stock tanks dug here and there, and a line of troughs along the yard.

Sitting a little uphill, the ranch house was built of heavy logs that must have been skidded in at least a dozen miles from the high timber country in the Little Belt Mountains. It was a huge sprawling affair, with junipers planted low around the walls and deep verandah porches. The shingle-roofed bunkhouse was over on the other side of the clean yard by a blacksmithery. Set to one side was a log stable for upward of thirty horses. Between the bunkhouse and stable fifty feet of rail fencing formed a stockade, divided up into a couple of horse-breaking and -working corrals. Surrounding the compound was the triple windbreak, tall cottonwood lined with willow and Lombardy poplar.

Cord's offhand guess was that this place would run somewhere in excess of five thousand head of mother cows, with a fair herd of horses. A dozen or so head of fine-looking saddle stock ran in a willow-lined pasture by a tank, solid strong animals, dark bay and high in the back. Cord could envy the man who owned this place, but still he wondered how greed could drive you when you already had the world.

Chi reined up abruptly, and Cord came up beside her. A bunch of shouting men were mobbed up in the ranch yard, and Cord felt a momentary jolt of alarm: he'd assumed that this bright spring daylight would be enough to keep Stringer's bunch out of sight, or at least out of action. Then Cord spotted F. X. Connaught, Bliss's dour foreman, leaning back against a wagon box facing the half circle of men, holding both hands up palm out for silence.

Cord and Chi rode on into the yard. The dozen or so men around Connaught wore chaps and worn boots, except for one older man with thin white hair wearing an apron: a cowhand crew and their cook, looked to be. Connaught called, "Silence! Every man will get to speak his piece by and by." It was some sort of meeting.

Off to one side, near another bunkhouse backed up to the corral and watching with some amusement, lounged the one-armed man Pincus and the light-skinned Negro called Sheeny. As Cord and Chi rode up, another cowhand called out, "The man cooked up his own trouble, and now he gits to eat the mess hisself." Other men muttered agreement.

Pincus and Sheeny straightened up at the sight of Cord and Chi. Pincus said something to the Negro, and Sheeny eased off to where a saddled horse was tethered to a corral rail. He mounted up and rode away to the north.

"Figure we know where he's heading," Cord muttered.

"That's all right," Chi said. "It's about time everyone got acquainted."

The white-haired cook wrung his hands. "Are you with us, F. X.?" he asked. "Will you represent our grievances to the man?"

But Connaught was looking over at Cord and Chi. He lowered his hands. One by one, the men turned and fell silent at the sight of the tall gunman and the dark woman, death and dreams materialized in their midst.

Their heads turned to follow as Cord and Chi rode up to the corral. Pincus came up as they dismounted and tethered their horses. "You are in our territory now," he said. "You like to take chances."

"Not me." Chi stepped out from between the horses. "I like sure things. Like if you don't step aside and shut your mouth right now, I'm going to hurt you. Bet on that for a sure thing, *pendejo*."

It must have reminded Pincus of the bad news Chi had conjured in the saloon. "See to you later." But he backed away, careful not to look toward the cowhands.

Cord kept half an eye on them. Could be they'd figure Cord and Chi as reinforcements for Stringer's bunch before anyone got a chance to explain differently. Cord didn't want any extra trouble; these men were innocent bystanders, and let them stay that way.

The cook said, "What the hell?"

Connaught looked past Cord and Chi. "Be at ease, lads," he said.

Cord turned. Mallory Bliss stood out on the porch of the big house. Beside Cord, Chi said, "Our man," and indeed it could have been no one else.

Bliss stood rigid, taking it all in, the hot breeze whipping his long black hair. He should have looked imposing, but Cord thought he looked rather lost. He was dressed impeccably in stovepipe pants, white shirt and collar, and a black vest. He wore no gun but carried his broad saber, leaning on it as a cane. Everyone stared back at him, as if his next word would name their fates.

"Sir!" Bliss boomed. He pointed the saber at Cord like a wand, stared at him for a long beat before turning to Chi, the moves practiced and theatrical. But he seemed to find Chi not exactly as written in the script in his mind, for he regarded her with widening eyes and nostrils. "And madam," he added, with a little bow of the head, lowering the sword. "Will you come into my home?"

Behind Bliss, posed there on his verandah porch, the logs were sided over with gray clapboard, and bright red shutters hung to either side of wide French-paned windows. Two intertwined rails of elk and deer antlers flanked the porch steps, gray monuments to the passage of time.

"You ever see anything like that before?" Cord said out of the side of his mouth.

"Not outside an opera house," Chi admitted.

Bliss stepped aside and made a great ceremonial gesture of welcome with his sword, bowing slightly at the waist and indicating the yawning ornate hardwood front door. The steps between the horn banisters were a half-dozen huge logs sawn in half, and the porch was floored with straight-grain tongue-and-groove cedar planks. All the wood was gleaming with clean varnish thick as melted candy. Bliss had read of the lives of rich men in his books and created this in the image of that dream. The upkeep must be endless, Cord imagined. He followed Chi up on the porch.

"Please enter," Bliss said. He leaned on the sword when he walked and swayed a bit. Cord had only seen him horse-back before and wondered now in what war battle he'd been hamstrung.

But then there were more immediate items at which to wonder. The castle of Mallory Bliss was luxurious in the overstuffed horsehide manner of some English country house, perhaps slightly distorted by the imagination of the man who built it but tasteful nonetheless and graced with every-thing wonderful that money could buy in this age and world. Cord saw teardrop crystal chandeliers, Empire furniture, oriental rugs like museum hangings strewn carelessly over the hardwood floor.

This front room was a library: three writing desks, deep leather reading chairs, and green-shaded lamps. And books, books climbing shelves on all four walls, reaching for the ceiling, more books than a man could read in ten lifetimes, every damned one of them bound in rich leather. This man must own half the books in Montana.

"What do you think, sir?"

What was there to say? "It's the damnedest house I ever saw," Cord said, and it was the truth.

Bliss took it for a compliment and stood beaming, as if he and Cord had never encountered one another before; as if Cord had not witnessed the hanging of Wee Bill Blewin, as if his right hand were as any man's. The man was crazy as the doctor had said, and true craziness made Cord very uncomfortable. His hand itched under the bandages.

"Savor it all," Bliss said, and he led them up the wide curving central stairway, through bedroom after bedroom, each decorated in a different scheme of colors and each with its private bath with walls tiled with delicately veined porcelain. The tubs were of stiffened rubber, and thick wolfskin mats were strewn about the floors.

Belowstairs Bliss ushered them into his wine cellar, cool and dry even in this unnatural spring weather. Ceiling-high racks, their feet settled into the clean white gravel floor, held hundreds of bottles of sherries, burgundies, and champagnes, resting side-angled in their pigeonholes.

"We have wine with every meal," Bliss said. "Fine wine from France."

"Imagine that," Chi murmured. She was not really impressed, but neither was she being ironical. For her, madness held fascination; Cord suspected she thought it somehow divine.

"I prefer to live as they do in Europe," Bliss said. "My people will see how rich life can be, and aspire to better themselves." He smiled fondly, as if these were sensible notions.

Upstairs, the hardwood floors of a music room glowed warmly in the light from huge windows. There were two pianos—*for Christ sake*, Cord thought, *two goddamned pianos*? And a harp, taller than most men, with music open on a stand before it. One end of the room was an atelier where someone had been painting with watercolors. At least there was a half-finished picture on an easel and a bowl of wax fruit on the windowsill. . . . Could all of this be merely an elaborate setting for a drama that took place mostly in the mind of Mallory Bliss? "You play the harp?" Cord asked.

"Oh, no," said Bliss, as if this were a reasonable question. "With these fingers?" He showed them thick callused hands. "Are you a music lover?"

"Not actually," Cord said. "It's just that someone damn near played the harp for me the other night."

Bliss frowned thoughtfully, as if such a mention was a minor faux pas at this time, like a fart at a formal dinner. "Come," he said generously, the gracious host willing to overlook. He ushered them on through a servant's door and they emerged in the kitchen. A chef in a tall white hat spun around a bit awkwardly and stood at attention. He held a chopping knife, and Cord smelled whiskey on his breath. "Carry on, Beaumont," Bliss said. The chef looked relieved. He threw open cabinets to show off his pantry: neat rows of cans with the distinctive label of Park & Tilford, capers and plovers' eggs, queen olives, canned truffles, mushrooms and meringues.

"Is all well, Beaumont?" Bliss said.

"Huh?" The chef wiped his mouth with the sleeve of his white jacket. "Sure." As Bliss led the way out, the chef gave Cord an odd wink.

They ended up back in the library, with its smoking stands, decanters of liquor on an oak sideboard, and everywhere the books. Chi settled herself into a chair, crossed her legs, and folded her hands on her knees. She looked as if she could get used to this sort of luxury quite quickly.

Through the translucent linen curtains of the front window, Cord saw the knot of cowhands around F. X. Connaught, pleading their discontent. Their mouths moved like those of players in a dumb show; no sound penetrated this room, no sound nor any barnyard dust or smell. Bliss had properly isolated himself from all the earthy doings that had put him where he was.

Cord turned from the window. "I would say they are fixing to walk out on you," he said to Bliss. "Hope you got a good plan."

Bliss said, "Sir?" and put on a bemused look. But then he went past Cord and pulled heavy brocade drapes across the window, shutting out the sight of mutiny and the brightness of the day. Cord wandered away while Bliss fussed with the drapes. Beside the biggest thickest reading chair in the corner, a volume rested on the table, a red ribbon marking Bliss's place. Cord picked it up and read the title embossed in the leather of its cover: *Little Dorrit*, by Dickens. Cord had read it.

"Well sir," Bliss said. "Tell me how you find my home."

Cord put the book down. "Must keep you busy," he said. "Just trying to remember what you've got."

"I have my people," Bliss said. "They are paid to remember."

"Servants," Cord suggested.

"Of course. My wine steward and butler, my laundress and seamstress."

Chi sat in her chair, smiling sweetly at this nonsense. That old kitchen hand, with the smell of whiskey and the chuck wagon still on him . . . "Where are these serving people?" Cord demanded. "Everyone got the day off?"

"They will be here soon enough," Bliss said serenely. "A Dutchman is coming to plant my gardens."

Cord threw up his hands. "What the hell are we doing here?" he said to Chi.

"Won't you take a drink?" Bliss sounded a trifle anxious now.

"You want to go?" Chi asked Cord.

"Yeah," Cord said. "Hell, I don't know."

"A drink, sir," Bliss said.

Cord whirled around and advanced two steps on Bliss. "Why the hell would I drink with you?" He shook his swathed hand under Bliss's nose. "This remind you of anything, you pixilated son of a bitch?"

Bliss squinted at the hand. "Will it be all right?"

"Yeah. That doesn't make me any happier about wearing this mitten. I am accustomed to having this hand available for certain activities."

"I have thanked God you were not hurt worse." Bliss went to the oak sideboard. "I will not abide the abuse of innocent men."

Cord snorted. "I got some bad news for you, Mister."

"Nor will I abide crime and thievery in my basin," Bliss went on. "Here rustlers receive their reward."

"Rustlers, strangers, anyone you happen on," Cord snapped. "That boy, Wee Bill Blewin—what was your big hurry? You could have made inquiries, see if he was telling anything like the truth. You could at least give a passing nod to something like law."

"Law and justice sometimes ride different sides of the trail," Bliss pontificated.

"Well, it beats me how in the hell you can set yourself up as judge, jury, and head hangman. Someone is going to fix your wagon real soon now."

"You?" Bliss said softly.

Cord laughed. He looked at Chi, serenely observing from her comfortable seat. "I hope it's true what they say about God watching over madmen," he said to her. "This bedlamite is going to need divine help."

Bliss gasped. Cord turned on him, prepared to toss a few choice words his way and get the hell out of there. But

Bliss's expression stopped Cord in his tracks. He looked stricken; the creases in his craggy weathered face quivered with some deep emotion. "Please," he said raggedly. "Take a drink and give me the chance to explain myself."

"Might as well," Chi said. Cord scowled at her, and she smiled back. "But make it a light one for my partner," she said to Bliss. "We don't want to get him started this early in the day."

Mallory Bliss's story began on the long six-month trail from west Texas north across the great open desert, and at first it was merely the usual tale of cattle-driving horrors: screaming animals swept away in melt-off swollen rivers, days of rain turning the world into a muddy hell, forever in the saddle with no sleep to speak of, and so on. Cord had trail-handed himself for more than one season, his first years away from home and out on his own driving cows to the Kansas railheads, and he freely agreed with Bliss: It was a miserable way to make a few dollars. Cord had hated it enough to turn outlaw.

Still, he didn't know what hard times in olden days had to do with anything. Chi, though, was paying attention, as if Bliss really had something to say. So she liked old loco men; maybe that was why she stuck with him, Cord thought wryly.

"We cut our way through fences when we had to," Bliss was saying. "Even back then so much of the free country was overrun. Nesters took claim to the best bottomland, then tried to charge for watering your animals. Some planted a crop right across the trail, traditional road that had been so long before them. They would wait in hiding for the cattle to muck through, then come out cussing and waving a shotgun and yelling for damages. We paid them damned little attention, I assure you."

They pressed on, Bliss said, he and Connaught, until they found this basin. He told how they lived in a tent the first winter and a soddy the second, caulking the cracks with packed snow. "We slept on mattresses stuffed with wild hay—Montana feathers, we called it," Bliss said, gazing off into his memories. "We lived on wild game and canned goods. It was a good time for young men."

"That's dandy," Cord said. "Get on with it, Bliss. What do you want from us?"

"I want you to understand," Bliss boomed angrily. "I fought for every damned thing I ever had. Storms roared down from Canada, driving cattle across the open country and covering the feed with snow packed hard and dense as tar. Timber wolves killed our calves. And the Indians, they were hungry as wolves themselves with the buffalo gone, helping themselves to my stock. Now," Bliss said, "we got the rustlers. Can you expect me to stand for it?"

"Anyone gets in your way, kill them dead," Cord said sarcastically. "You got the right."

"Good men and women are welcome here. Thieving trash will be purged."

"Along with a few innocent men."

"They are all guilty of something. Those kind are always guilty." Bliss took a big swig of his drink. "When we came, this was savage wilderness. To tame it required savage methods."

Bliss turned abruptly away. "That night," he said in a low voice, "I had to give them Blewin, but I was able to save you. So you see: I have not lost all control. I will not surrender my domain to ruffians." He reminded Cord of a child, bragging aloud about not fearing ghosts while passing the graveyard late at night.

"And that brings us to your good friend Mister Stringer," Cord said. "There is the sort of righteous fellow you are looking for to fill your town. You don't mind *him* helping himself to your beef. Is that right?"

"We will rid ourselves of the rustlers, and after that Stringer will be unnecessary."

"Glad to hear everything is crackerjack." Cord put his glass on the sideboard. "We've had our drink and some swell palaver." He glanced at Chi. "Guess we'll be running along."

Chi was watching Bliss. He ran his hand through his mane of dark hair and said nothing. "All right," Chi said to him. *"Bueno."* She stood.

Bliss leaned forward, his body quivering, as if he were standing on the brink of a great abyss and were being drawn by demonic force toward its depth. His face was contorted with something like pain. "Help me." The words sounded strangled.

Cord suddenly hated the man—for what he had done to him, for drawing them in this way, for his madness. "Stringer means to take it all," Cord spat. "He is going to steal everything you have, and not a damned thing you can do to stop him."

"Cord!" Chi said reproachfully. "Stay or go, but stop abusing the *viejo.*"

"He tried to abuse me."

"That's done with, far as he goes. You know where to find your vengeance."

Cord squared his shoulders and drew a breath. "All right," he said to Bliss. "I can get over the part about nearly being hanged—could be you saved my life, if you don't look it over too closely. But you and I are never going to see eye to eye. I believe the things a man does have consequences, and you must face them and deal with them. You think you are exempt from such responsibility." Cord stared into Bliss's mad eyes, striving for contact. "It's a notion that is going to get you killed."

"Yes . . ." Bliss rubbed his eyes with the tips of the fingers of both hands, as if changing his mask. "I have a proposition for you, sir," he said, his voice almost controlled again.

"Everyone does," Cord said. "What's yours?"

"I offer you both employment, as stock detectives in this basin."

"You got plenty enough detectives already," Cord said. "They are likely riding your range right now, detecting which pilgrim to lynch next."

"Talk straight," Chi said from her chair.

"You have helped me to come to my decision," Bliss said portentously. "I will dismiss Stringer and his men."

"Pay them off," Cord said, "and you figure they'll ride right out of here, happy as clams?"

"There is no longer a place for Stringer in my scheme," Bliss said. But maintaining the fiction of his control cost some effort.

"But us you can use."

"Ten thousand dollars," Bliss said.

"Twenty," Cord said. "You can afford it."

Bliss nodded slowly. "Twenty thousand dollars, for peace in my basin. That is fair."

"Pay up."

Bliss looked to Chi. Maybe her odd gentleness had given him to believe she was his ally. But she nodded her agreement with Cord.

Bliss removed a half-dozen books from a shelf to reveal

a wall safe. He spun the dial, carefully blocking their view with his body. Inside were stacks of currency. Bliss counted out a considerable pile, shut the same, whirled the dial. When he turned, the money was clutched tightly to the front of his vest. "How can I be sure?"

"Don't dare ask that question," Cord snapped. "Hand it over."

Bliss did as he was told.

"You buy gunfolk like they were yard goods and expect trust and loyalty?" Cord gave the money to Chi. It disappeared under her serape. "We could ride out of here this day, take this money and whatever more you've got, and not a damned thing you could do about it. You are too deep into trouble, and without us and plenty of luck to boot, you will never get out."

Chi stood. "You done?"

"Almost." Cord stabbed a finger at Bliss. "Remember one thing more, old man," he went on. "You brought the trouble to this basin, you and your greed and your bad dreams of being Caesar. So from here on, you be damned careful what you say to me. You can trust me all right— trust me to hurt you badly if you do another thing I don't like."

Bliss gaped at Cord. Likely no one had talked to him this way for some years.

"Anything you'd care to add?" Cord said over his shoulder.

"Looks like you covered it," Chi said mildly. Bliss stood there, his lips slightly parted.

Cord said, "*Adios*" and opened the front door. The sounds of men talking drifted back in. "The only thing that I hate is the siding," he said in a low voice. "A dozen or so guns against two."

"Maybe three," Chi said.

"Huh?" Cord said. "You got something to tell me?"

But she was not listening to him. Cord peered across the yard in the direction she was looking and thought, *Well, hell*. "Never mind," he said aloud. "It can wait."

Chapter Eight

THE CLOT OF MOVEMENT OUT ACROSS THE prairie past the windbreak resolved itself into men on horseback, more than a few. "We could beat them on out of here," Cord said on the porch, half thinking aloud. "Pick our own spot later on."

"It wouldn't look good," Chi said.

Cord wondered if she were kidding. But she looked serious enough, and so they stayed where they were.

The cowhand meeting was finished. Over in front of the bunkhouse, men were tightening cinches, strapping on saddlebags and rifle scabbards, tying down bedrolls. They were leaving for good, and who could blame them? Dust raced before the approaching riders, driven by the hot wind.

Connaught stepped up on the porch. "They have asked for their time, every man of them," Connaught told Cord and Chi. "I could not dissuade them."

"Why should you, *viejo*?" Chi asked.

Connaught peered over his shoulders at the riders on the plain. "There was a day when I would have gone to Hell for that man."

Cord counted eight riders in the bunch.

"I risked my life time and again for him," Connaught said. "But always against nature, never guns. And this as well: He has changed in ways I cannot countenance. All our early days, we wished only to use the land the way God meant. Now he must rule."

Cord could hear hooves drumming the sod, saw Sheeny's brown face among others as the horsemen circled around toward a break in the trees.

"This basin will explode," Connaught said. "The fuse has been lit, and only a fool would keep his seat atop the powder keg. We are finished." He shook his head. "I'd best go tell him."

"*Buena suerte, viejo*," Chi said.

"Thank you," Connaught said. "Luck to you, too, lady."

Horses came thundering into the yard; they had been ridden hard. Stringer wasn't hard to pick out, in the blocky fighting boots with the steel-lined toes. He was biggest and rode at the head of the bunch, and when he raised his hands they lined up behind him, Sheeny and the other six. Dust swirled around their horses' legs before settling.

"Riding on, boys?" Stringer shouted at the cowhands. They stood frozen where they'd been. "Good idea—we got no need for you." His tone went mean and bullying. "Get moving!" he shouted.

Stringer stared blackly at the cowhands all the time they got themselves horseback, turned their animals, and rode out in a ragged line. He waited until they were gone before turning slowly to Cord and Chi, as if he had been sure they'd stay put until he was ready to deal with them. Cord was thinking odds again and groping for ideas. The only one that came readily to mind was to let Stringer make the first play. He had most of the guns. Stringer folded his hands over his saddlehorn and smirked for a good long time.

"Cut him out of the pack," Chi said from the side of her mouth. "I'll cover the others."

"Hope so," Cord said.

Stringer rode to the center of the yard, staring down at Cord all the time. "How's your hand, son?" he inquired. He climbed off, sidled away from his horse. Cord stepped down from the porch. Chi moved off to the side where she could keep an eye on all involved.

Stringer removed his hat and wiped a sleeve across his brow. His bullet head was mostly bald, his scalp freshly reddened by the new spring sun.

"I should have killed you first chance I had," Stringer said. "But I decided you weren't worth rocking the boat over." He flung the hat away, moved his hand carefully to near his gun butt. "Guess I was wrong."

Every eye was on them except Chi's, and Cord felt acutely self-conscious. His hand: damn but he hoped it would not betray him.

"Well, that is one mistake I can fix easy enough," Stringer said and slapped for his gun.

On the porch, Chi fired first.

Cord drew at the same moment, but he rushed the move, and as he brought up the gun he fumbled it and it arched away from him. Cord dove for it, and whatever Chi had shot, it wasn't Stringer, because his shot came off right as rain, slicing the air where Cord had been.

Cord stared at his gun, a yard away in the dirt. Stringer

thumbed back the hammer of his weapon and lined down on Cord.

Behind Stringer someone loosed a strangled animal cry. Stringer spun on his heel, keeping half an eye on Cord. Up in the barn loft, Pincus rose from behind a bale, a rifle in his hands: a moment before it had been aimed at Cord, ready to kill him dead if Stringer bungled the job. Pincus half stood, twisting as he stumbled over the bale, and lurched out of the loft. He struck the hard-packed dirt like a sack of winter spuds.

Stringer said, "Well, son of a bitch," and turned back to Cord as he scuttled to his fallen Colt.

Chi put a shot into the dirt at Stringer's feet. "That's enough gunfighting for this afternoon," she said. "You boys can have your fun some other time."

"You afraid of a fair fight?" Stringer said.

Chi shrugged. "All right, *cabrón*, go ahead and kill him. Still won't be a fair fight, because I will shoot you down an instant later." She showed Stringer her gun. "See if I won't."

Cord's gaze was riveted on Stringer's hand and his thumb, poised on the hammer of his revolver, and Cord thought, *Jesus Christ, he does not believe her*. Cord looked into Stringer's deadly scowl. Cord's left hand was around the butt of his own gun, but his arm felt weak and fluttery: He was staring at his death and could not move, a character in his earliest worst nightmare.

A gun went off.

For an instant not a soul moved. Then one of the horsemen behind Stringer slumped forward onto the neck of his animal, a gun hanging from limp fingers. The man's weight slid over out of the saddle and he landed on his back in the dust. The front of his blouse was soggy with blood where the bullet had come out. Another bushwhacking son of a bitch out of the way, Cord thought.

"Let's everyone drop their guns," someone hollered. "Just for the time being."

Cord got to his knees. Over the riderless horse he made out the newcomer, astride a big white horse. His name was Nick Oakley, and he had partnered Wee Bill Blewin on and off. Cord knew him and hated running into him again.

Oakley worked the lever of his rifle. "This is a Winchester repeater," he called, "and I got the drop. Take out two—three of you boys at least, shoot you in the back before you ever get to see my face. Who wants to gamble it won't be him?"

Handguns dropped to the dirt, and men muttered in low voices. "You too, Baldy," Oakley called.

Cord raised his gun. "Do it," he ordered. He sounded unconvincing even to himself. "Come on now," he added, and felt conspicuous and foolish.

Stringer dropped his gun.

A sickening wave of humiliation washed over Cord. He detested this moment, kneeling in the dust in front of all these men, especially Oakley. His heart thumped in his chest, and only force of will kept his hands from trembling. He had been horribly frightened, and he detested that worst of all.

Cord climbed to his feet. Not another man moved, and every eye drilled into him. Cord imagined their disdain, exaggerating it in his mind until it seemed to fairly sear his skin. Cord looked through the line of men at Nick Oakley.

Oakley was a few years younger than Cord, somewhere in his early thirties, slim and dark and tanned with wise handsome features. He wore black leather gloves, and when he raised his left hand and touched two fingers to his hat brim, he gave Cord a smile in which contempt was all too real.

"Let's get moving," Chi said. Her gun was still on Stringer.

Cord could not stand the expression on Oakley's face, not on top of the fright that had jolted him, and knew he must act, right here and quickly.

"Let's ride," Chi said.

Nick Oakley smiled at Cord.

"No!" Cord said, much louder than he meant. Who was he hollering at? But that wasn't actually the point. Staring down Stringer, Cord put his Colt away and unbuckled his gun belt, lowered it to the ground and moved away.

Stringer smiled brightly and did likewise. Cord glanced at Chi. She nodded to him with the slightest smile; she understood. Cord managed to work his bandaged right hand into a passable fist. "Keep a sharp eye, Oakley, now that you've dealt yourself in."

"I'm still deciding who to root for," Oakley said laconically. But Cord saw that Oakley kept his rifle in position for quick restoration of order if necessary.

Stringer put up his dukes and grinned his mean grin. "By rights, I ought to tie one hand behind my back," Stringer said. "Guess I won't." He closed, circling slowly, playing for an opening.

Cord feinted right and went in with his left.

Stringer caught the punch on his big ropy forearm and hit Cord squarely in the jaw, driving his fist from the shoulder.

Cord spun around and fell, instinctively breaking the fall with his right hand and taking a jolt of sting through it for his trouble. Tears of pain smeared his vision. He blinked them clear in time to see Stringer swing back a leg, and then the battering-ram–lined toe of his fighting boot coming at his face.

Cord rolled away, and the boot sole brushed his hair. He rolled another turn and to his feet, shaking off the grogginess.

Stringer closed again. Cord ducked under his roundhouse right and followed with a combination to Stringer's belly. The bastard's stocky trunk was hard as wood, and Cord's right hand throbbed. Stringer grunted sour breath in Cord's face.

Stringer dropped his shoulder and hit Cord in the stomach, lifting him to his toes and bending him over. Stringer swung from his knees and caught Cord under the point of the chin. Cord staggered back. Stringer waded in, jabbed Cord in the face again. Cord's head swam with pain, and it was difficult to get his arms up. He went back another step, and while he was off-balance Stringer hit him in the face a third time, pile-driving his big meat hook hand into Cord's mouth. Cord sat down hard in the dirt.

Stringer laughed and came on.

Cord crab-scuttled back. Gravel worked under the dressing and pressed into his palm. Stringer plodded after him like a grizzly on a scent.

Cord forced himself to focus: Nothing but this battle existed, no Chi or Oakley or anyone else, and no pain. The world was tiny, only him and Stringer, and as that world contracted, only one could survive.

Cord's back hit the side of one of the watering troughs. He got himself to a sitting position, took a deep breath, concentrated on getting his feet under him, levering himself upright to carry on the fight.

Stringer was over him, eclipsing the daylight. "This has

been a lot of fun," Stringer said, "but I got to be going now."

Stringer swung back his arms and one leg, poised for a moment with all of his weight brought to bear, and launched a terrific kick at Cord's breastbone.

Cord threw himself to the side, and Stringer's weighted boot slammed into the side of the watering trough with tremendous force. Planks creaked and splintered, and Stringer's weight carried him through into the water as it sluiced out, its pressure throwing him off-balance.

Cord swung around and chopped the edge of his left hand into Stringer's shin. The big man howled, instinctively jerking up his leg. Cord threw his weight into Stringer's other leg, tackling and holding on, lifting Stringer and throwing him forward onto his hands and knees.

Cord flung himself on Stringer's back, his weight driving Stringer's face down into the sudden pool of mud surrounding them. Cord hit Stringer in the base of his skull. Stringer moaned.

Cord climbed up Stringer's torso, got hold of his head by both ears. He rammed Stringer's face down into the mire, again, a third time, a fourth. Cord raised Stringer's head once more, bending his limp neck backward.

Cord gasped. He lay Stringer down on his cheek so his nose was out of the puddle. A long run of shuddering shook Cord's body, and he had to let it pass before he was able to climb raggedly to his feet. He jerked Stringer over on his back. Stringer's nose was broken and bleeding, his face a hash of mud and blood and purpling bruises.

Chi watched Cord from the porch, and in her soft brown face was compassion and understanding. Another massive wave of trembling ran over Cord like an earth tremor. He had nearly killed a man with his hands—would have if he hadn't stopped himself. It seemed a descent into an extraordinary sort of savagery, quite beyond what Cord believed himself capable of.

Mallory Bliss and F. X. Connaught stood on the porch before the great oak door. Connaught looked saddened, but Bliss was pale and drawn. Cord felt as if he had been caught performing an unnatural act.

Cord wiped mud from his face. "Let's get out of here."

Chi brought over the horses. "Okay," Cord muttered. "Fine." He swung into the saddle and rode down the line of men. In their faces Cord saw a mixture of puzzlement, curiosity, and respect, and he felt a little better. He reined up and looked at Oakley. "Come along."

Oakley frowned.

"Not a word," Cord said. "Just shut up and do as you are told."

Oakley looked past Cord at Chi. Cord jerked his bay around and let everyone have his back. Behind him he heard Oakley say something in a low voice and fall in line. Cord spurred the gelding and led them away from there and out into the bowl of grassland at a hard gallop.

Chapter Nine

"**L**ET'S NOT TALK," CORD SAID. "IT MAKES my mouth hurt."

"You pretty sure nothing's busted?" Chi asked.

Cord worked his jaw with his fingers. Though it was sore, and his upper lip split and his lower torn by his own teeth, the bones seemed in one piece. He spit out a trace of blood.

"I guess," he said thickly. "The more I get hit in the head, the harder it gets."

"That's good," Chi said solemnly. "Man who gets in as much trouble as you, he needs a hard head."

Cord unfolded his hands from over his face and sat up. From this little rise by the road, they could see miles in any direction, and were safe from ambush as they would be anywhere this side of Helena. The ranch headquarters to the north was about the same distance as the windmill to the south. Their horses were grazing on the green spring grass nearby.

Oakley sat crouched on his haunches to one side. He had listened quietly to Cord's account of the hanging of Wee Bill Blewin. Now Cord took his pouch from his shirt pocket and tossed it to Chi. "You got any questions?" he asked Oakley.

"I do." Oakley worked a blade of grass between his front teeth. "You think you will run out on me if we get boxed in?"

Cord forced himself not to look away. In fifteen years of hard adventure, Cord had committed few acts he now regretted. Of them, the one involving Nick Oakley he regretted most.

"No," Cord said firmly. "I owe you."

"Yeah, you do."

"I'm thinking on ways to pay you back."

"What's between you two is for later." Chi handed cigarettes to Cord and Oakley, put one between her own lips. "Right now we got business to see to. Wee Bill was telling the truth, wasn't he? You two haven't taken to rustling, have you?"

"Yeah," Oakley said. "Meaning no." He took a light from Cord, cupping it within both hands against the hot wind. "Wee Bill told the truth about us working for this Canaday hombre. We'd been on the trail for better than a week, and that empty cabin with the corral looked like the place to rest us and the stock for a day."

Oakley blew out a thin stream of smoke. "An hour after we drove them in, I caught someone snooping around the corral. He howdied me friendly enough, and we talked horses some, but me and Billy didn't like his looks. We'd heard the stories of night riders in these parts, same as everyone, but after encountering this fellow, we were more apt to credit them."

Off across the prairie the whitetails grazed among the placid cattle. "We figured a way to avoid trouble was to ride in to town—we'd seen the road sign—and present the bill of sale to the sheriff. Turns out they ain't got a sheriff. What they got is a saloon."

"Handy," Cord said.

"I like saloons in the afternoon," Oakley said dreamily. "I like the cool and the quiet, and the old smoky smell, in the air and in the whiskey. This was a funny little place, run by a bartender who thinks he's a librarian, and an adventuress who thinks she's a doctor."

"With a snake who thinks he can strike through glass."

"So you been there. Anyway, I drank more than somewhat and didn't eat anything, and by and by I flopped in one of the rooms they got upstairs. I woke up maybe three in the morning, sober and worrying about Wee Bill. I should have done that some earlier."

"You didn't know," Chi said. "You weren't against the law."

"Law is for who makes it," Oakley said. "And that's not ever us."

Cord crushed out his cigarette and shredded the butt. "No law wants us for anything."

"Guess you are sitting pretty then, Cord," Oakley said. "Anyway," he went on, "I took a look at the burned-out cabin and Wee Bill's body," Oakley said, "and I rattled hocks out of there. I'm not so proud that I didn't take time to bury him proper, but I was scared. One of them saw me, I was dead. I thought I couldn't take them all on."

"But you've changed your mind."

Oakley shook his head. "I still don't think I got a chance—not by myself."

"Now wait up," Cord said. Partnering wasn't a proposition he'd expected from Nick Oakley, not after what happened. . . .

"Hear me out," Oakley said, quietly but firmly.

Chi gave Cord a look and he shut his mouth.

"I served some time once, Cord. You maybe remember." Oakley put a sarcastic twist on it. "But nowadays no law has a call on me neither. So why should I let hooligans run me like a monkey?"

"Where did I hear that lately?" Chi said, smiling at Cord.

"There is more," Oakley said. "I told a man in Wyoming I would do a job, and I shall do my best to keep my word. And this Mallory Bliss had my partner killed. I can't let that pass. Would you?"

"Never mind me," Cord said, a little sharply.

"Try this," Oakley said. "Maybe we used to ride outside other men's laws, but we acknowledged some rules. Now comes this Bliss, thinking he is God Almighty and his word is scripture, rules be damned. So what does he get: these night riders, and the worst sort of chaos."

"And you propose to rectify it?"

"Someone ought to," Oakley said earnestly. "Someone must."

"He is right," Chi said. "You want to settle, Cord, you got to be willing to do your part as a citizen."

"Huh?" Cord said. "What's that?"

"The right thing," Chi said.

Cord stared off north at Bliss Ranch headquarters, serene as its grazing cattle, yet about to explode hot as the wind. "Okay," Cord said wearily. "What do you propose?"

"First of all, I mean to get that old man."

"It's Stringer you want," Cord said carefully. "Same as me."

"I don't think so."

"I was there, damn it, and I say Stringer is your man."

"Bliss hired him."

"And then Stringer got out of control—and it was him who killed your partner."

"How'd you live through the fun?" Oakley asked.

"I was born lucky," Cord snapped. "Now I'm telling you: Stay away from that old man."

Oakley looked at Cord for a long moment, then glanced at Chi. Chi nodded, barely moving her chin. Oakley shrugged. Nice how she could calm boys down so easily, Cord thought with some resentment. She had a way with all the men. . . .

"All right," Oakley said. "Since we're letting our hair down, I got one more piece of news. While I was panicked and on the run, heading toward the North Gap, I nearly overcame a herd of horses and cows being driven that way. I circled around. After a time I stopped at a roadhouse in a little town called Geraldine. The bartender told me herds had been passing through for a couple of weeks."

"And Stringer and his boys were driving them, probably up into Canada," Cord said. "That's not news to us."

"Did you know Stringer was gathering them in gulches in that breaks country near the river up along the north-western rim of this basin?"

"Didn't know," Cord said. "Don't much care."

Chi understood. "Maybe your stock is up there," Chi suggested.

"Not yet," Oakley said. "That was them in the horse pasture at the big house, watching Stringer try to beat Cord's brains out."

"I thought they might be," Cord said. "Couldn't tell for sure. There was a moon that night, but I was interested in other animals."

"I mean to take back my horses before they are moved out," Oakley said. "Anyone want to come along?"

"We got other troubles begging to be looked into," Cord said. "I hurt Stringer pretty bad, least I hope so, but he's not dead and he won't run, not with all those guns to back him. Once he's able—tomorrow at the latest, is my guess— he and his bunch'll come riding for me."

"There is the idea," Oakley insisted. "With Stringer down, tonight is the time for getting back my horses."

"I got other fish to fry." Cord touched at his split lip with his bad hand. "I got to conserve my strength," he added. "What I got left."

"I'll ride with you," Chi said to Oakley.

"Say what?" Cord barked.

"We can take a look around at the setup anyway." Chi turned to Cord. "Stringer is too beat-up for gunfighting tonight."

"Maybe," Cord said. He wished she would not go with Oakley, but she knew that.

Oakley stood and went to his horse. "I'm going to keep moving," he said. "I trust no one tied to Bliss, and that goes for those two back in Enterprise. I want my back against no walls."

Oakley swung into the saddle. "I'll be at that windmill around dusk." He nodded to Chi. "See you." He gave Cord a cool, neutral look, and rode off.

"Come on," Cord said. He could not keep his voice entirely free of annoyance. "I think I might be able to use a drink."

"You sure could use a bath," Chi said. "You decide about

the drink." She knew how Cord got around whiskey. Sometimes his timing was awful, but right now she decided not to worry about it.

They rode in silence for a time, the hot thick wind rolling over them. "You told a lie, *querido*," Chi said after a time.

"How's that?"

"Bliss was the one, wasn't he? He ordered Wee Bill's death."

"How'd you know?"

"You can't keep secrets from me," she said lightly. "You try, but it never works."

"I changed the story," Cord admitted. "I don't know—like you said at the big house, I guess I know who has got to pay." He gave it some thought. "Bliss is crazy—there is no point in looking for satisfaction from him. He would never get it. It'd be like trying to teach a duck to read."

"He is lost," Chi said.

"That's no excuse." Cord shook his head. "But still, I reckon that somewhere the killing and vengeance has got to stop."

Chi nodded, as if he had passed a small test. "But not until after Stringer."

"You bet," Cord said.

Chapter Ten

CORD JERKED BACK. FIONA COBB GRABBED HIS
wrist, twisted it so his hand was once more faceup on
the table, and splashed more witch hazel over the hash of
scratches and blisters on his palm. The sting of the liniment
brought involuntary tears to Cord's eyes.

"Hold still," Fiona Cobb said.

"I bet that smarts." Richard Carlisle leaned on the bar,
a bottle of gin and a tumbler close to hand.

"I will show you smart," Cord warned. He drank the rest
of the bourbon from his shot glass, using his left hand. The
whiskey was starting to touch him. Well, that's what it was
for. . . .

Back in Enterprise from Bliss's ranch, he'd pulled off
his muddy clothes and flopped down in one of the rooms
upstairs to sleep away his aches and pains and most of the
afternoon. When he awoke, clean clothing from his sad-

dlebags was laid out, and somewhere beyond the open door, Chi was singing in Spanish. Cord wrapped a sheet around himself and followed the sound to a bathroom at the end of the hallway, where he found Chi dumping the last of a bucket of hot water into an iron tub. She was in a gay mood and offered to scrub his back. He shooed her out gruffly; the business with Oakley had come back to mind by then.

Now, downstairs in the saloon, Fiona Cobb worked the medication into his hand. "You ought to take better care of your body, Cord," the doctor said. "You are not as young as you once were."

"I don't need a surgeon to tell me that," Cord said. He ran his free hand through his damp hair. It wanted cutting.

Chi appeared from the back door and smiled across at him.

"Drink?" Carlisle offered.

"Not right now," Chi said.

Cord looked out the window, and sure enough, up the street at the base of the windmill, Nick Oakley sat his horse, its white hide turned golden in the twilight. She would know he was there; she always knew those things.

Chi stopped at the table. "You be careful," she said to Cord.

"Take your own advice." It sounded surlier than he'd meant.

"I won't be long." Chi reached down and ran a fingernail over his hurt hand. "*Querido*," she said gently.

"Sure," Cord said. "Go on." He watched her unhitch her mare, swing gracefully into the saddle. The last of the sun shot its rays between the peaks of the divide, far off west beyond the roofline of the library.

"Your partner is an extraordinary woman, Cord," Fiona Cobb said.

"Yeah," Cord grumbled. "Sometimes a little too extraordinary for my taste."

"You'd prefer she'd stayed here with you."

Cord looked away; he did not wish to see them ride off together. "You want a drink?"

"Yes, thank you." Fiona Cobb began to unravel fresh bandages from a roll. Cord carried his glass and hers to the bar. Fiona Cobb was drinking whiskey and water.

The rattlesnake slept in its jar at the other end of the bar, near the connecting door to the café. Carlisle refilled Cord's glass from a bottle of Jim Beam and Cord put the liquor down neat. "'Nother, while I'm here," Cord said. "Save me a trip." Carlisle poured again.

Cord carried the glasses back to the table. "There's times she goes her own way," Cord said.

Fiona Cobb sipped at her drink. She wore a long dark velvet dress cut low across the bosom.

"Me, too, sometimes," Cord went on. He gave Fiona Cobb a lickerish smile, but she didn't get it, or chose to ignore him. "She doesn't take orders well. People try to tell her what to do, she gets awfully wrought up."

"Give me back your hand," Fiona Cobb said. She started to rebandage it.

Cord was three drinks into what he suspected would be a pretty fair session of packing down the juice. Fiona Cobb and Richard Carlisle, near as he could tell, had something of a habit; most always they were somewhere close to a drink. Yet both seemed more or less sober, anyway pretty far from falling-down drunk.

"That must be something to see," Carlisle said. "Your partner wrought up."

"You don't want to be at the other end of it. Take it from

someone who knows." Cord took his drink in a quick series of swallows.

"Another?"

Cord shrugged, and Carlisle refilled his glass. But then Cord decided that maybe this was a bad time to be a complete moron and let the bourbon sit. "You mind if I make myself a sandwich in that café of yours?"

"You can have a steak if you want. Beef is what we got plenty of."

"Sandwich is okay," Cord said. "I want to stay upright for a while, but I hate to ruin a good drunk with too much food."

"I'll get it," Carlisle said. "It makes me feel useful."

Cord tapped a finger on the tabletop. "Tomorrow, maybe the next day, Stringer is coming in with his boys. I'm who he is mainly mad at, but he'll want you out of his hair as well, so if he gets me, you-all are next. Plan he's got doesn't call for any doctors or librarians."

This time Cord sipped his drink. "I am going to try to stop him. Right then is when you are going to be real useful, 'cause you are going to side me. Both of you."

"Me?" Fiona Cobb tied off the bandage. "I have little experience with guns."

"You point at what you want to shoot." Cord extended the forefinger of his left hand at her and cocked his thumb. "You pull the trigger. Boom," Cord said softly.

"Take it easy." The heat in Carlisle's tone surprised Cord. Carlisle paused in the entryway to the café and turned to Cord. "No point in throwing needless scares into people."

"You scared, Mister Librarian?"

"Yeah. That's right."

"You got to think about it." Cord felt the drunk stirring inside him, trying to get loose and cause mischief. "You

got to know what you are going to do when the trouble
starts and there is no more time for thinking."

"Go out after dark," Carlisle suggested. "Find Stringer
in his weakened condition and kill him."

"Just like that?"

"Why not?"

"You ever kill a man in his sleep?"

"Of course not."

"Then you do it," Cord said. "It'll be a new experience
for you."

"What difference does it make how Stringer dies?" Carlisle said. "The man is a murderer a dozen times over. Who
cares if he sees the man who makes him pay for it?"

"I care. I'm the one who'll know, the one who will wake
up at three o'clock on the odd morning, sweating ice water
and trembling like I was damned. There is some physiological psychology for you, Doc," Cord said. He looked
back to Carlisle. "A fight will come, sure as sunset, and
you just might be a part of it. Hope to God you can hold
up your end."

"I guess we'll see what happens," Carlisle said. He went
into the kitchen.

Fiona Cobb took a long pull from her whiskey and water.
Cord let his drink alone for a moment. "The snake," he
said, breaking the twilight silence.

"Richard?" Fiona Cobb was surprised.

Cord turned back to her. "The one in the jar. I hate
snakes."

"Few people like them."

"I knew a woman who did, though. Had one for a pet,
the kind that squeezed little animals for food—a constric-
tor." Cord was half talking to himself now. "Used to be in
the carnival."

"The snake or the woman?"

"Both. They did a dance. Anyway, this woman I'm thinking of, when she touched that snake, played with it, she got—"

Fiona Cobb leaned forward over the table. "Aroused?"

Cord studied Fiona Cobb's breasts. "Something like that."

"What the hell?" Carlisle stood in the connecting door with Cord's sandwich, frowning. "Did I miss something?"

"Freshen my drink, please, Richard."

Carlisle came over and put down Cord's plate. "Why not?" Carlisle took Fiona Cobb's glass behind the bar.

The sandwich was that morning's breakfast beef between two thick slabs of the wheat bread, with horseradish and mustard. The first bite reminded Cord he was hungry. "Damned good," Cord said. He looked toward the bar. "I been riding you a little hard. Sorry."

"Decent of you," Carlisle said, still a shade miffed.

"You bake the bread?" Cord asked Fiona Cobb.

"*I* bake the bread," Carlisle informed him.

"Good," Cord mumbled. He was tired of spatting.

"Cord was telling tales, Richard." Fiona Cobb watched Cord eat. "About women and snakes. He likes the former and hates the latter."

"I will tell you a tale," Cord said abruptly.

Fiona Cobb and Carlisle looked at him curiously. Cord pushed away the unfinished half of his sandwich and got out his makings. "Can either of you roll a cigarette?"

Fiona Cobb took the pouch and began to worry open the drawstring.

"There is a man and a woman in this tale," Cord said, "and a snake as well. Nick Oakley and my partner are the man and the woman."

Cord took the cigarette Fiona Cobb handed him, lighted

a match under the lip of the table, and fired up, exhaled smoke.

"I am the snake," Cord said.

Carlisle brought bottle from the bar and joined them at the table. "I like a good tale," he said.

"As it turns out," Cord said, "me and Chi and Oakley, along with that Wee Bill Blewin, once partnered up. Or meant to, anyway."

Carlisle refilled Cord's glass. Cord was not sure why he was telling these people things—except he'd had enough to drink and had to tell someone, clear it out of his head. He pursed his lips and blew out a smoke ring and peered through it into the long ago.

The first part of the tale went way back in Cord's career to days before he partnered with Chi, when he was just one of a gang and Nick Oakley was another. Oakley was sixteen years old, looking to be tough but hanging on mostly as a horse holder and camp cook. One time another of the gang, an old outlaw hand, bullied Oakley, and Cord, hardly past twenty himself, stood up for the kid. There was a fight.

"I won," Cord said. "There was Toad Matson, sitting in the campfire and spitting teeth, and there was Oakley, looking at me as if I was his hero. But he had it wrong: I only never liked seeing the helpless get pounded around. I would have defended a dog same way, least in those days." There was no edge in being someone's hero; it made them expect you to act certain ways, and when you didn't live up to the image they'd invented, the admiration could turn to hate. . . .

The gang broke up without making any real money, and life meandered on. By and by Oakley got partnered with Wee Bill Blewin and Cord with Chi. Then, a half dozen or so years later, on a hot sweaty summer day in Denver, Oakley and Cord ran into each other once more.

Oakley recognized Cord, though Cord likely would not have recognized the younger man. In his mid-twenties, Oakley had grown good-looking, and self-assured without being cocky; there wasn't any of the dim worshipful kid to him now. With Wee Bill, he had come to a measure of outlaw renown, and it sat on them gracefully enough.

Cord and Chi should not have been in Denver. Those days they were wanted in one state, two territories, and by the federal government, so they made a habit of avoiding cities. But Denver happened to be where they had stashed their savings, two thousand dollars, all the real money they had in the world, in an account under the name of Epheseus Palmerson in the First Denver Reliance and Trust Bank.

At this point in the story Carlisle laughed. "I thought you two were in the bank-robbing business. I'd expect you'd sooner hide your money under a rock in the desert."

"Only in the dime novels," Cord said. "Big city banks are safe as they come. They have big city vaults and big city guards, and big city cops come after you when you've done the job. Only a rube would think of trying to knock one over."

The idea was to get in, withdraw the money they needed to get by for a while, and haul ass back to the territories. But then they ran into Oakley and Blewin.

Oakley was no longer panting in Cord's wake, but he accorded Cord some frank regard. It was honestly earned: Cord and Chi had gone some further in outlawing than Oakley and Blewin—more people were after their hides anyway. Oakley expressed his respect forthrightly. He had an idea for a job, and he offered them in on it.

"This particular job required more than two people,"

Cord said in the saloon. "Oakley reckoned I was someone he could trust."

"Sure," Carlisle said. "You taking his side against bullies and all, you'd be aces in his book. So," Carlisle said. "Were you someone he could trust?"

Cord winced at that part of the memory. "Keep still," Cord said. "Maybe you will find out."

"The suspense is delicious," Fiona Cobb said. Her glass hid her face as she drank, so Cord could not tell if she were serious.

Nick Oakley had in mind a robbery, but not a bank: his target was the Railway Express Agency office at the northwest end of Sixteenth Street, near the Union Pacific terminal. Wee Bill had been hanging around the barrooms down near the rail yards—"Looking for opportunities," as he put it. A couple of nights earlier Wee Bill had gotten an express clerk very drunk and had come away with a lesson in a new and specialized corner of commerce.

When you were a big mining magnate and had all the gold and silver the greediest man could ever want, the clerk told Wee Bill, you sought new ostentations. To this end, the mining men occasionally shipped ingots of the purest metals from the company mines in places like Leadville, Aspen, and Ouray to artisans in Chicago, to be fashioned into fine jewelry. In three days a large consignment would return by express to decorate the thick wrists and wrinkled necks of mining men's blubbery wives.

The person who took delivery at the express office was the local jeweler who brokered the deal. There was nothing to the job, Oakley said. They needed only to wait until the jeweler picked up the pieces, accompanied as per his habit by a single guard. Then they would take the goods away from him. Easier than any bank, Oakley insisted: no safes to open, no citizens getting in the way, no secret alarm buttons or hideaway guns.

"Well, I didn't like it." Cord paused while Carlisle poured him another stiff drink. There was a lamp on the table now against the encroaching darkness, and Cord held his glass to its light as if examining the whiskey for impurities. "As I said, big city cops tend to be smarter and more tenacious than country sheriffs. And the weather bothered me as well. It was way too hot for that place and the time of year."

"Like this basin about now."

"But this was the big city," Cord said, "and it was having one of the worst heat waves anyone could remember. It gets hot enough in the city, and people start to go crazy. Bet that's in your book, Doc."

Nor did Cord like messing with mining magnates. They were different from the garden variety of capitalist: Most of them started out as raggedy-assed prospectors themselves and had hung on to some goldfield toughness and tenacity. They were likely to get pissed off at having their goods stolen and try to do something about it—like hiring a goon squad of killer Pinkertons to run down the thieves like dogs.

Finally, Cord and Chi had a rule against stealing property. It had to be converted to cash money, and that meant involving other people and bringing in all sorts of new and unacceptable risks.

But Oakley had an answer to each of Cord's objections. Men were men, he insisted, whether police, Pinkertons, or plutocrats, and facing down men was part of the outlaw game. Then Oakley put down seeing omens in the weather as superstitious claptrap. Cord knew better, but still, Oakley was making sort of a dare and Cord was on the spot.

As to the goods, Oakley went on, they would simply melt the jewelry down. That made no sense to Cord; it was the expedient answer of the shortsighted. Fine jewelry was worth twice as much as the raw metal; if they were going to melt it down, why not go up into the gold country and rob some foreman's safe? Cord did not mean to take the trouble to steal jewelry in the big city merely so they could melt it down.

"No deal," Cord said. "That's what I told them."

"Ah, but something changed your mind," Carlisle guessed.

It was Chi: she had overruled him, told Oakley and Blewin they would think it over. In private, Cord reiterated his arguments, and though she did not refute them, she would not concede. She was in one of her stubborn streaks, for reasons Cord could not fathom. She was going in on this job with Oakley, and Cord be hanged. She walked off on him, leaving a half-finished drink on the bar.

Next time he saw her was a couple hours later, through the window of the fancy restaurant. Cord was looking in from the sidewalk, and Chi was at a table with Nick Oakley, smiling and chattering, gay as a parakeet. Cord wanted to go in and break some furniture with Oakley's head, then slap Chi around.

"The thing is," Cord said in the Enterprise Saloon, "if I hit her, she'd kill me, then or any day to come."

"Do you blame her?" Fiona Cobb said.

"Not a bit. You-all may have figured this out or not, but fact is that we've never shared a bed. Chi and me go our own ways when it comes to close companions. That's the rule, which doesn't mean I was always happy with it."

"Like lately," Fiona Cobb said shrewdly. "You are very fond of that woman."

Cord blinked and focused on the doctor. She was a puzzlement for a woman. "Never mind that," he said. "I am talking about another time. Her with Oakley irritated me into some drinking, so when I went to bed, I slept hard enough not to know if she came back to the hotel before morning. So maybe she did, and maybe she didn't."

The next morning at breakfast, Cord found himself watching Oakley and Chi like a hawk for signs of something between them, cursing himself silently all the while for acting like an epicene cuckold in a Gilbert and Sullivan operetta. So Cord had finally agreed to throw in on the deal; it was preferable to the alternative of Chi running off with Oakley.

There was nothing complex to the plan. Chi would distract the jeweler and his bodyguard for the moment it took for Cord to get the drop on the guard. Oakley would be the second gun, demanding the loot, while Blewin stood by in an alley with rope and their horses. By the time the two men got untied and ungagged, the four of them would be miles out of town and heading north for Cheyenne. All they had to do was wait for the UP train from Chicago two mornings hence.

For Cord, the waiting was not easy. The damned heat was no help, and the second night Chi definitely did not sleep in her own room. Cord made damned certain and then confronted Chi. She was compromising the job, he insisted.

"You ought to be ashamed," she reproached. "Spying on me." That was the end of that talk.

Restlessness came over Cord like a storm front. He fetched his bay from the livery, thinking maybe a ride would settle him. He was crazy, and sitting still would drive him crazier yet. He rode northwest on the post road toward Boulder.

About halfway along, fifteen or so miles out of Denver, Cord came upon a little roadhouse saloon. It was plain and nameless, but the rude interior beckoned, cool and calming.

"I thought I would have a little drink," Cord said. He held out his glass toward Carlisle. "In fact, I think I will have one now." Carlisle poured. "Put it on my tab," Cord said.

A big kind-faced man tended that Colorado roadhouse bar, and a couple of solid old citizens stood sipping at beer. They turned out to be retired from farming, Cord found out when he got to talking to them. After a time and some drinks, Cord stopped thinking about Chi and that unctuous woman-chasing son of a bitch Nick Oakley. He had some more drinks.

When the old men excused themselves for supper, it occurred to Cord that he'd best move on back to Denver. A late afternoon breeze would cool and sober his system.

"Sounds like the right idea," Carlisle said in the saloon.

"Oh yes," Cord said, "but then I had one that was even better: Buy a pint bottle of bourbon for the road. One of those brilliant drunk ideas, one of those notions so pregnant with trouble they are nearly miraculous." Cord studied his crooked distorted reflection in the globe of the coal-oil lamp, watched himself grin sourly.

He found Chi and Oakley having their dinner in the saloon, cozy as ticks. He sat down to join them, smiling a big smile that dared one of them to say he couldn't. When that didn't work, Cord tried a few out-of-line remarks. Chi tried to get him to shut up and eat something. Nope, Cord told her; he was drinking supper that night. Then do it at the bar, Chi snapped, and leave sober people in peace.

Cord nodded grandly and swaggered over to the bar. Time for another drink anyway. When she finished eating, Chi came to stand beside him. She told him there was no reason for him to act this way, that it wasn't fair to the rest of them. She reminded him that he must keep his nose out of her love life and stay in shape to do what had to be done the next day.

Chi spoke her piece softly and kindly, and Cord came back at her with a string of loudmouthed insults. Chi's expression darkened, but before she could put him in his place, the man behind Cord at the bar put his hand on Cord's shoulder.

Cord turned around. This old boy was big and broad and had the smell of the railroad stockyards to him. Cord smiled pleasantly at him. He was drinking with a chum, about as big and scowling about as meanly.

"You bothering this lady?" the big stockhand asked.

"Right you are," Cord said agreeably. "Now piss off."

Cord got in the first punch, an ice-hard right to the jaw that set the man down on the floor. But his buddy got his hands around Cord's neck and rode him down. He was sitting on Cord's chest and clawing for Cord's eyes when Oakley rabbit-punched the man in the back of the neck with both hands. By that time the first stockhand was back in the fray and Chi and other patrons were starting to take a hand. The brawl became general, and items got broken.

After not too long, police whistles sounded. Chi got Cord to his feet and had him off near the back alley exit when the cops came in. They grabbed for whoever was handy and came up with Oakley right off. Cord lurched in that direction to help, but Chi jerked him up short.

"*Estupido*," she hissed. "There is federal paper on us." She was right, of course: They would not get a week for disorderly conduct but ten years in the penitentiary.

Cord let her walk him out the back door.

They went straight to the hotel for their things. There they found Wee Bill Blewin. He listened to their story and allowed that he'd stay around to see if there were anything he could do for his pard. "You'd best get moving," he said, looking at Cord. "Guess you've done all you could."

They rode most of the night, and by morning Cord was sober and full of misery. His head hurt, and he felt guilty as all hell.

In the Enterprise Saloon, Cord pounded his bandaged fist on the table hard enough to make the bottles sway. "Son of a bitch." A few inches of bourbon remained in the one Cord had been working on. He peered blearily at Carlisle and Fiona Cobb. "I guess Mister Oakley's got a right to be sore."

"What happened to him?" Fiona Cobb asked.

"They found an old charge outstanding from when he was a kid and passing through the city dead-broke. Petty larceny—stealing a chicken from a butcher's yard. The limitations were run out on it, but the judge figured Oakley owed them time anyway, so they charged him with every-thing they could—public drunkenness, disturbing the peace, resisting arrest, and so on—and gave him nine months in the workhouse. They let him out after six, but he did hard time."

"It's always hard time," Carlisle said, sounding as if he were speaking from experience. Cord was too drunk to remember if they'd been pacing him—for sure they'd been drinking steadily—yet both seemed to have their wits about them.

"It was purely my fault that he ended up in jail." Cord pushed his glass toward Carlisle. "Can't expect a man to forgive or forget that."

"You can't undo it now," Fiona Cobb pointed out.

"Maybe not."

"Other men have done worse," Carlisle muttered, peering thoughtfully into his glass.

"But not me," Cord said urgently. "Not before and never since." Cord held his fresh drink. "Chi was sleeping with Oakley, sure—but *I* was her partner, before, then, and always. When the police came running and it was him or me, she didn't even think about it. I'd been brooding for two days and acting like six kinds of moron, but she never hesitated."

"Could be she grabbed whoever was closest," Carlisle said.

Cord struck the table with his fist again.

"Careful of your hand," Fiona Cobb said.

"My hand." Cord slugged back his drink. He knew, even besotted, that he was nearing the end of that period of seeming lucidity and heading toward the big crash. He pushed back his chair and stood, swaying some but able to stay upright without holding on to anything. He smiled foolishly at Carlisle and Fiona Cobb, peered around the room, and lit on the snake, asleep in its jar on the far end of the bar.

Cord went to it, bent with hands on thighs, and stared at the reptile blearily. It lay motionless, eyes open but oblivious. Carefully, tentatively, Cord lay his good hand on the glass.

Nothing happened for a good thirty seconds. Cord imagined he'd see the rattles go first, but he was wrong. The snake twitched and struck, shooting his fangs at Cord's hand as if lightning-struck.

Cord jerked his hand back and swore. The snake withdrew lazily, recoiled itself.

Carlisle laughed.

Cord turned on him, stabbed out a finger. "Can you do it?"

"Once in a while," Carlisle said. "When I've drunk enough."

"We all have, for tonight," Fiona Cobb said. "Let's close up, Richard."

Carlisle gave no sign of hearing her. Cord said, "Come on, take a turn. Don't be a pill."

Carlisle came over, and Cord stepped back out of the way. Carlisle looked at Cord and then at the snake.

"I'm still fast," Cord said. "One thing I can do drunk nearly good as sober."

"What?" Carlisle licked his lips and set his hand on the bottle near the snake. "Stop babbling and let me concentrate."

Cord drew his Colt and fired. The bottle exploded under Carlisle's hand, and the noise of the gunshot echoed like death in the room. Carlisle screamed and leaped back, slipped on broken glass, grabbed for a chair and upended it as he went down.

The snake slithered off the bar and dropped to the floor, its rattles chattering madly. Carlisle scuttled back away from it. Cord started to laugh. The rattler turned in Cord's direction, and in his drunkenness Cord remembered that he hated snakes.

He shot the rattler in the head, and when its body continued to twitch, Cord put a couple of shots into its writhing length as well.

"That's enough," Carlisle said weakly. "Jesus, Cord."

Fiona Cobb was standing beside Cord, touching his elbow. "I prescribe some sleep, Cord." She ran her fingers along his forearm. Her touch was soft and warm through his shirt. "Are you going to be all right?"

Cord peered down at the tops of her breasts. "Yeah," he said thickly. "Always. All my life."

"Good," Fiona Cobb said. She held on to him a moment longer, and Cord thought he saw something in her expression. She bent, picked up the dead snake without ceremony, and flung it out the back door. "Good night, Cord," she said. Cord watched every step as she went out.

Carlisle stood, brushing bits of broken glass from his trouser legs. "Nice goddamned trick," he said.

"It got your attention." Cord was staring at the open front door. "She is a job of work."

"Forget her."

Cord smirked at Carlisle.

"You can be a real muttonhead when you are drunk, Cord," Carlisle said. "Anyone ever tell you that?" It was true enough, and Cord's jaw dropped. "Wind the clock and put out the cat," Carlisle said. "I'm going to bed as well."

"You gonna lock up?"

"From whom? The night riders want whiskey, they'll kick the door in. Who else is there?" Carlisle opened the front door. "Sleep upstairs in a bed or here on the floor. Whatever suits you." He went out.

Cord took his glass back to the table and emptied the rest of his bottle into it. That made an even quart. A nice round number. He tried to roll a cigarette but gave it up for a bad job. He sipped the drink to make it last, and after a time got a new stupid idea.

Outside in the street's darkness, the hot breeze still blew, and the blades of the windmill made a faint whir, like crickets. The Milky Way swept brightly overhead, and down the street a light burned in the side window of Fiona Cobb's place.

Cord went along an alley, circled round back of the saloon, and cat-footed along the ditch, coming into her lot from the back, past the privy. He crouched and snuck up under the window. He remembered the touch of her hand on his arm and grinned, thinking: a woman mostly alone in the middle of nowhere, her husband long gone . . . Cord took off his hat, raised his head with exaggerated drunken care, until he could see above the windowsill.

Fiona Cobb stood in her bedroom in her chemise, her hair down, her thighs smooth and white in wicked-down lantern light. She clung tightly to a coatless, collarless Richard Carlisle.

Cord ducked down and froze in position for a long moment before easing away from there, praying to the gods who watch over drunks not to humiliate him utterly by allowing him to make a noise. He moped back to town feeling astonishingly sorry for himself; was this the depth to which his life had descended, peeping in the windows of ladies' bedrooms?

He did not have to worry about it long. He barely managed to make it up the stairs to his room and flop onto the groaning bed before the world went away.

Chapter Eleven

"*QUÉ PIENSAS?*" CHI ASKED.

"*No se,*" Nick Oakley said in a low voice. "We can try to make that corral and run them horses, but I'm not married to the notion. I'd like a better idea of where everyone is and how many are going to want to chase after us."

Crouched in the cover of the windbreak trees, they had a clean view of most of the ranch headquarters. They had waited some hours out on the open range for the moon to set, but the sky was still bright with great washes of stars; there was nothing to do for that, though. The big house sat stolid and dark.

With the cowhands gone, Stringer and most of his men had come in from their hideout in the breaks and taken over the bunkhouse. Two were smoking on the porch, a blond man and a big-bellied short man who had been among the riders they had encountered on their last visit here. The bunkhouse was lit from inside, and the front door was open, but no one seemed to be stirring. It was well past midnight.

The hot dry breeze from the west whipped at their hat brims as Chi and Oakley hunkered among the willows. This weather was unnatural and somehow foreboding; Chi sensed in it a portent of disaster.

Her dark thoughts were pierced by a terrible noise, a great loud inchoate roar from inside the bunkhouse. It could have been the brutal sound of an animal hurt and enraged, but it was not. "*Madre Dios*," Chi breathed.

Oakley let out a rasp of air, as if he had been holding his breath.

The voice howled again, semiarticulately this time, a stream of pointless unconnected obscenities, Stringer bellowing out his pain and rage. Chi wondered how the mad Bliss sitting alone with his harp and his pianos, liked the sound of savagery.

"Take a closer look?" Oakley suggested.

"We better." Chi drew her Colt from under her serape. "Before I lose my nerve." The first-floor light in the big house went out.

Oakley put a gloved hand on her shoulder. She looked back at him. "Just wanted to say thanks," he mumbled. "Good to have at least one gun with me."

"Don't think too badly of Cord. He's got a bandaged-up gun hand and a man coming to kill him, and not much he can do for either but wait. You got to consider the ways that would make a man feel."

"You worried for him?"

"No," Chi said, without hesitation. The most immediate potential for deadliness was right here before them, and she did not mean to split her concentration fretting on another fight on another day. "But I'd hate to see him dead," she said softly.

They'd spoken little on the ride out, and surely not about the long-ago two-night Denver love affair. Not that it was a touchy point, at least for Chi. She'd had a good enough time; she'd liked Oakley then and did now. He reminded her a bit of Cord.

Cord: When this was over, he and she had to have some serious straight talk. She smiled in the night. Maybe it wouldn't be talk; maybe she would just find his bed one night.

Stringer shouted at his demons again. Chi cleared reflection from her mind. This was no time to resolve her life.

"Look there," Oakley said.

A lamp had flared in the front upstairs room of the big house. Now curtains parted, and Mallory Bliss stood silhouetted behind the window. The mullions crisscrossed his figure, and he looked for all the world like a prisoner.

"Come on," Chi said.

They stayed in the cover of the trees as they circled behind the house. They paused behind a privy near the rear rail of the corral to survey the yard, but no one was in sight, nothing moved save the milling horses. "They're Canaday's, all right," Oakley confirmed in a whisper. Besides his half-dozen, another eight or ten animals, the night riders' saddle mounts, stood quiet in the night, sleeping or nosing each other's flanks.

"Be ready," Chi said, and broke for a quick dash through the shadows to make the rear of the bunkhouse. She tipped her sombrero back so it hung from its neck thong, eased up to peer through a dusty window.

She was looking into a dim dormitory with accommodations for maybe a dozen men to sleep and snort in a row of close-set beds along either side. Gear hung from thick tenpenny nails driven into the log walls.

An entryway at the far end of this room opened into the lighted bull pen in the front half of the building. Four men were playing cards at a rickety table, passing around a bottle. Chi took in a few ill-used chairs, part of a shelf strewn with books and magazines, and through the open front door the shapes of the two men on the porch. Everyone seemed at ease for now—everyone except Stringer.

He lay on one of the bunks in this near room, in britches, suspenders, union suit and bare feet. On an upended crate beside him sat a bottle of whiskey, two-thirds full, and a coal-oil lamp.

In its yellow light, Chi could see that Stringer's coarse features were not improved by the beating Cord had administered. His nose was shattered, bent over onto one cheek, and his lips were puffed and caked with blood. One eye was blackened, and a cut ran from above it across his high forehead to his balding pate. Sheeny sat in a chair nearby, feeding him from the bottle.

Stringer gathered himself, half sat up on his elbows, and screamed again, cursing out his rage into the night. The cardplayers exchanged significant glances and went on betting and tossing chips; this raving must have gone on long enough for them to have become inured. Stringer yowled like a leg-snared coyote. One of the cardplayers pointed to his own temple, rolled his eyes, and rotated his finger. Could be, Chi thought, listening to the echo of Stringer's wounded cry; Cord had pounded him hard enough to knock him crazy.

Sheeny held the bottle of booze and Stringer gurgled down an inch. Or could be he was just drunk. Whatever, right now he was a man two or three cartridges short of a full magazine.

Stringer shoved aside the bottle. He swung his legs off the bunk, so Sheeny had to push his chair back out of the way or be kicked. Sitting up, Stringer seemed to come a ways back toward himself. "Where's Bronson and Turk?" he growled. Before the black man could answer, Stringer hollered out the men's names. At the card table in the front room, a man stopped in the middle of the deal, looked at the other players quizzically.

The blonde and the stocky man came in from the porch. Stringer was pulling on his boots.

"We're riding," Stringer said to the floor. His voice was ominous with unnatural anger. "Bronson!" he shouted again.

"Right here," the blonde said. He shot a glance at Turk. "I'll tell the men to be saddled before sunup."

"You tell the men to be saddled in fifteen minutes. Some-one see to my horse."

"It don't make any sense," Turk muttered. The men in the front room had gathered near the entryway, peering into the dimness.

"Shut up!" Stringer stood and looked at the others. "Any man says any damned thing to me is dead, any damned thing at all. Who disbelieves me?"

"No question," Bronson said blandly.

Chi watched from the shadow of the window.

"Where is my damned gun, Sheeny?" Stringer said. Sheeny lifted Stringer's gun belt from a nail, held it for Stringer to step into.

Stringer worked the buckle. "Bastard killed my kid brother," Stringer said, staring awfully at Bronson and Turk as if accusing one of them of the deed. "Shot him down like a he was a snake. He's a back-shooting son of a bitch."

"That's him," Bronson said.

"Never could have touched Luke or me in a fair fight,"

Stringer went on, his tone puerile. "Fair fight, he'd be twice dead already."

"What you said," Bronson answered, like the chorus in a Greek play.

"He wants to fight dirty, we will show him how it is done," Stringer said. "We are going into that Enterprise town—all of us," he snapped at the men in the entryway. "We are going to roust Mister Gunfighter Cord out of his bed, and we are going to strip him down, and once that is done, I am going to start doing him."

"Then there is the woman," Turk said, with broad insinuation.

Chi made a mental note of this moron.

"She has got to watch," Stringer said. "After that, do what you want. I got no use for her."

"That Oakley?"

"He's run out, if he's smart. If not, we'll make him wish he had."

Behind her, Chi heard Oakley mutter, "Damn," soft and ominous.

She spun around, staying low and her gun ready, to see one of Stringer's men stopped short halfway to the outhouse and facing Oakley. Chi had the dead drop on the night rider from the side, but she hesitated a beat, knowing that the sound of the first shot would be the starting signal for mayhem.

The night rider slapped for this gun. Oakley's was already out, and no more time for hesitation. Oakley fired.

Chi turned back to the window before the night rider hit the dirt. She broke a greasy pane of glass with her gun barrel, squeezed the trigger.

Stringer, facing her direction, could move fast, drunk or hurt or no. He twisted out of her line, grabbed up the lamp, and flung it at the window. His aim was high: The lamp hit the lintel and shattered. A tiny drop of hot oil seared Chi's cheek as she ducked away.

Oakley was in the corral. Chi raced toward him, ducking and dodging in anticipation of gunfire from the bunkhouse window, but none came. As she vaulted the fence rail, she caught a glimpse of angry flames licking out the rear window, sparks popping as wisps of bark on the cabin's logs ignited. Around front, men were shouting, Stringer's bellow overlaying the gathering chaos. A few random shots split the night. Stringer screamed, "Get the bitch."

Chi pushed in among the animals, wide-awake now and skitterish from the noise and fire, rearing and snorting and whinnying. Oakley jerked up the gate latch, swung it wide. A spotted gray horse swung around, its flank knocking Chi away. She grabbed at its halter, swung up bareback.

Oakley caught a horse and clambered atop it, screaming at the other animals, whipping with his hat and the halter reins. A knot of men came around from the direction of the bunkhouse, and Chi threw a shot their way. Someone hollered like he was hit. The gray tried to buck, but she jerked it back to attention.

Up ahead, animals broke for the open corral gate. Chi hurrahed, heading the rest that way. By then the horses had pretty much gotten the head of where running space lay, and they streamed for the gap in the fence, knocking against the posts on either side. A rail fell to the ground. Hooves pounded the hard-packed dirt of the yard, and dust rose in the hot wind.

The dry logs of the bunkhouse were burning by now, flames shooting twenty feet into the night. Stringer screamed, "Stop them horses!" A few men raced toward them, waving their arms and firing into the air, but they were moments too late. The horses were running hard and panicked.

Chi lay low on the gray's neck and fired twice at the knot of shapes silhouetted against the raging fire. Ahead of her, Oakley got off a shot and someone cried out above the general roar of noise. Chi aimed more carefully, picked a standing target as the gray came last through the corral gate.

Chi fired, and at that moment the gray reared and plunged sideways. Her shot went high and wide, and she just managed to grab for the animal's mane. She slid feet-first to the ground but held the horse, jerking its head as she vaulted onto his back once more. The horse half reared again, and there in the darkness and dust, in front of and below her, Chi saw one of the men, his pistol in both hands and throwing flame as he fired.

Chi shot him in the chest, and as the man went backward, the gray bolted, trampling over his body before plunging away into the night. Chi threw a last shot toward the flaming bunkhouse as she raked the gray from shoulder to flank, laying out flat and shouting in the animal's ear. Out ahead Oakley had pulled up and was giving her cover fire. Past him, horses fled in various directions, bounding and plunging over the starlit range.

"Let's go," Chi hollered as she came past. Oakley jerked his horse around and followed at a dead gallop. A few shots pursued, and then the firing stopped. They were out of range of gunfire, but they could still hear Stringer's roaring curses, rolling across the prairie like spring thunder.

A half mile out, the shadow of a gully creased the plain. They reined up, fast walked the horses down into the cover of the little dry wash. Theirs were tethered in a copse of chokecherry bushes. They left the gray and the horse Oakley had ridden and walked their saddled animals down the draw a ways.

"What the hell?" Chi muttered. The gully narrowed here just before its mouth, so she could not see over the range. But Oakley, a little ahead where the draw came out at the stage road, had remounted and sat staring back in the direction of Bliss's ranch, his mouth agape.

Oakley's face was lit by an eerie orange-red glow. She heard him mutter, "Holy Mother of God."

Chi swung into the saddle, rode out beside Oakley and into the unnatural radiance.

The bunkhouse had been consumed quickly. It gave off more smoke than flame now, a collapsed pile of charred logs.

The firelight that washed across the prairie to them came from the big house, Bliss's great elegant castle. The shell of the two-story structure was intact for the moment, but flames came from every window, licking, and grabbed for the darkness. As they watched, the big oaken front door buckled outward, fell from its hinges. From behind it, above the fire's roar, came eerie atonal music as the strings of the harp and the pianos stretched and whined with the heat. The canopy over the front verandah crashed down, like a trapdoor swinging shut.

Then, for a long moment, the entire huge block of house seemed to sway in the hot wind, a bit this way and a bit that, the massive beams of its frame creaking enormously. When it went, it was like an implosion, the walls falling in on themselves like those of a card house, sparks mushrooming into the air to be swept downwind in a thick wave.

"Bliss?" Chi murmured to the wind. *"Qué pasa?"*

"For right now," Oakley said, "let's worry about us."

Chapter Twelve

SOMETHING WAS WRONG. TROUBLE HAD COME into the air, like the sudden drop in barometric pressure foretokening a storm. Malevolent wraiths hovered all about. Cord opened his eyes and stared up at the ceiling's blankness, waited for the dream to fade. It would not.

Still drunk, he decided. He remembered where he was: on his back and fully dressed, except for his gunbelt, atop the bedclothes in one of the rooms of the Enterprise Hotel, above the saloon. The curtains were open and starlight flooded in so he could see well enough around the room. There was nothing special beyond the usual furniture, nor anything menacing here, but neither was he drunk. Not absolutely brick-cold sober maybe, but sober enough to take care of business. It hadn't been more than a couple hours past twilight when he'd plowed off to sleep; judging from how he felt, he'd passed a decent interval in the sack since. Cord wished his watch weren't busted.

He was not drunk and he was not dreaming, and yet something was absolutely not right. His gun and belt were folded on the night table beside him. That was instinct stronger than the worst booze-up: Do not risk rolling over and shooting off your foot, but keep your weapon close to hand. Cord heard a faint crackle, like tissue paper wrinkling.

Cord sat up slowly, but he felt well enough, though he could not be completely sober, because the hangover was not yet upon him. He reached for the gun belt and froze with his hand upon it.

The starlight in the room was tinged the slightest shade of red-orange.

Cord rose and went to the window, mechanically strapping on the belt, working the buckle awkwardly with his left hand.

Miles off to the northwest, flames etched a thin line between the ground and the night sky. Cord gasped. He turned, threw the door back against the wall, hit the stairs running, thinking first of the horses and then of Fiona Cobb and Carlisle, thinking survival.

Out in the street, the hot wind blew the first fine flakes of soot into his face as he ran against it. The ash was gritty on his lips. Cord was halfway up the windmill's ladder, fifty feet off the ground, before he remembered that heights made him dizzy. But this was high enough to see: The threat was worse than he had imagined, about as bad as it could be.

The vanguard edge of the fire, driven before the wind, was at least a mile wide and widening. Any hope that it would somehow miss the town was fond, outside of a miracle. It was coming, sure as hell, and compared to a range fire, hell was a temperate climate.

Cord backpedaled down the ladder, working his feet and good hand carefully. He was frightened, and there was no point in falling to his death. There would be plenty enough good ways to die on this black night.

Cord hit the ground and ran for the livery. He'd seen two prairie fires in his life and vividly remembered the horrors of each. One had flared in south Texas, on open range grazed by the first ranch he ever worked as a kid away from home. This was nubbly scrub country with not so much to burn but little water either, and though the flames were smaller, they were no easier to stop. The ranch boss ordered steers slaughtered and their carcasses dragged between two mounted men, ropes binding the legs of the dead beeves front and back and looped around saddle horns. One cowhand rode before the flames, the other on the burned-out side, in a galloping attempt to smother the fire. Cord could smell the burning cow flesh in his memory.

In the livery he found his bay and two other horses, Carlisle's and Fiona Cobb's, stalled side by side. They had not yet caught scent of the fire. Cord dragged tack from hooks, went to work fast as his hand and a half would allow.

Two seasons after the Texas conflagration, the drive Cord was riding with, ten men and twelve hundred beeves, came through the aftermath of a great fire in far southern Kansas. There was no way around; the few pilgrims they came upon, fleeing with what belongings they had saved, reported the ground was black for fifty miles in either direction. Immediately when the cows crossed the river separating grass from ash, their hooves churned up clouds of soot, dense enough to blot out the sun's color though not its heat. The grit covered men's skins and animals' hides, until the riders were black as fifty-dollar poker chips. Despite the neck-erchief over his mouth, Cord's lungs filled with the ash, and it ground into his nose and mouth and eyes, and his tears turned the dirt to mud that glued his lids shut.

They knew from past drives that there was another creek some good way ahead and nothing they could do for that either except pray that the wind did not shift. But it did, and when the parched cows caught scent of the water, they took off as if they were whipped. They ran for miles, burning off meat in a mad stampede that could not be headed, thousands of dollars of beef weight evaporated into thick stinking air.

Cord tightened the cinch of the bay's saddle and mounted up, leading the other two horses. He ducked under the livery's double door and rode into the street. The glow to the northwest was brighter; it would be. He did not know what he meant to do with the horses, but they'd die for certain in the livery, screaming and kicking down their stalls. They might make it, though, if he did, if he could figure out some island of refuge. . . .

Cord swore aloud. Even if somehow the fire passed them by, there would still be Stringer and his gang. Cord did not expect that the fire had gotten them; more likely Stringer started it, in some mad fit. He would wait it out and come in behind, picking through the ashes for Cord's bones and guns, ready in case he'd survived.

All right, he decided, first things first. Cord led the horses down the street and around the corner, halloing Fiona Cobb's house as it hove into view.

They must have been heavy sleepers; Cord had to pound on the front door for a full minute before Carlisle swung it open. "What the hell?" he sputtered. He wore a union suit and an angry countenance. "You are still drunk."

"Right," Cord snapped, "and look there."

Carlisle saw the horses then, saddled and grazing in Fiona Cobb's dooryard. He stepped out to the path, looked off where Cord was pointing.

Carlisle gasped.

Fiona Cobb appeared in the doorway behind Carlisle. Light from the hallway behind her made her long white nightgown diaphanous, and Cord could trace the curves of her figure beneath it. Her hair was down, and in the fire-tinged starlight she looked lovely. "Come in," she stammered.

"I'd like that," Cord said. "But right now I don't have time."

"We've got to get out of here," Carlisle said.

Cord shook his head. "You can't outrun a fire that size. It's faster than any animal, faster even than the wind that's pushing it."

"It must consume a vast amount of oxygen," Fiona Cobb said, thinking aloud. "It would create a vacuum before it and rush in to fill it."

"What do we do?" Carlisle asked.

"I got one good idea," Cord said. He looked around, checking his recollection. It could work. The yard around the house, surrounded on two sides and part of a third by the ditch, lay low as the surrounding ground, maybe lower in spots. . . . "Get some britches on, Carlisle."

"What . . . ?"

"Just do it," Cord barked.

Fiona Cobb stepped aside to let Carlisle back in. "How can I help?" She sounded solid enough; Cord hoped she would not break when the flames charged down on them.

"Picket those horses to the porch. Get a rope on them if

you can, strong as you got." Cord pointed back toward the windmill. "That tank full up?"

"We keep it that way."

Carlisle came back out, shrugging into his suspenders. "Get dressed and wait for us," Cord told Fiona Cobb. He grinned wryly. "Wear old clothes."

Ahead of them, as Cord and Carlisle dog trotted back up the street, the line of fire was no more than a few miles beyond the little knoll where they'd buried Wee Bill Blewin. Five, ten minutes and no one would ever find his grave again. The wind clawed at their faces, thickening with soot. Carlisle shouted, "Well, what is the plan?" His words seemed to be coming from the far end of a long tunnel.

By then they were in front of the mercantile. Cord gestured. "Get shovels, axes, buckets, burlap sacks, whatever you can find. Pile the gear out here. Dump flour and sugar if you must for the bags—this whole place will be burned to the ground before the hour is out anyway."

For a moment Carlisle stood where he was, and Cord thought he was about to argue. But then Carlisle said, "Your partner..."

Cord stabbed a finger at him. "Get moving!" Carlisle stumbled into the mercantile, coughing a little. Cord headed up toward the windmill. What about Chi, out at the ranch with Oakley? What had this fire to do with them and their plan for stealing back horses? Answers didn't matter if you could do nothing about them....

Big pully wheels controlled the headgates to either side of the big tank at the windmill's base. They were half-open and some rusted, and Cord felt a moment of panic; the wind carried some of the fire's heat now. Cord threw his weight against the first wheel, felt it budge. More water began to sluice through the gate feeding Fiona Cobb's ditch. Cord strained, and the wheel gave some more.

If Chi had run into trouble, it was over by now. A wave of terrible hopelessness sapped at Cord's strength. He drew a deep dirty breath. She could be all right; getting out of scrapes whole was her specialty, or he would not have let her go. *Let her go?* She did what she wanted. Anyway, there was still his own hide. He could still live. Cord heaved at the wheel, keeping that thought central.

The blade of the axe bit deeply into the base of the trunk of the cottonwood sapling, setting shivering waves of pain through Cord's bad hand. The cut was most of the way through the tree, and when Cord threw his shoulder against it, it broke free and splashed into the water. It was the last one; the rest of the windbreak around the back and sides of Fiona Cobb's house was already down. Cord dragged the leafy trunk around downstream, jammed it into the narrow ditch where the rest of the cut trees formed a rough dam.

Behind it, the ditch was brimful and overflowing into the low yard around the house. A sheet of water mostly covered it now, no more than an inch or two deep. Cord hoped to God it would do.

He could hear Carlisle and Fiona Cobb shouting to each other, but he could no longer see them, or anything but the outline of the house, through the thickening smoke. He soaked his neckerchief in the water, tied it over his nose and mouth.

Carlisle was on the roof, slapping down wet burlap sacks that Fiona Cobb handed up. As Cord came around the house and caught sight of him, Carlisle stamped on a spark as it landed. The horses stood tied to the porch post, hock-deep in the water.

Carlisle climbed down, coughing. "What now?"

"Fill those buckets. Pray for rain." And hope, Cord added silently.

Soot clouded over everything. The flames were no more than a half mile away now and closing fast, their roar now audible, loud as some great infernal engine. Hooves pounded nearby, and Cord whipped out his gun. Bawling cattle came stampeding out of the south end of the main street and raced out onto the prairie, the little herd that had been grazing near to town among the whitetails. Far behind them, other animals screamed. Somewhere out on the prairie, cows were afire.

Carlisle came out of the house with two rifles, propped them on the porch. Fiona Cobb had changed to a baggy pair of jeans and a man's flannel shirt. More animals approached but off from the west. Cord spun that way, looking for targets.

Chi and Nick Oakley rode out of the smoke.

She leaped her mare over the ditch, perfect in the saddle. Oakley's jump was not as smooth, but he made it. Cord felt immense relief.

Chi sat her horse a moment and looked around, then smiled down at Cord. "Looks like you know what you are about with an axe, working ditches," she said. "It'll come in right handy on that new place of yours."

Cord was abruptly aware of himself, sleeves rolled up, sweating, and leaning on the axe while he caught his breath. It wasn't funny. None of this was funny.

He flung the axe aside. "What the hell happened?" He was staring at Oakley.

Oakley shrugged and climbed down, took Chi's horse when she dismounted and led them over to the other animals.

Carlisle stood there on the porch, his arm around Fiona Cobb's waist.

Cord listened while Chi told him the story. He tried to imagine the great house burning, and somewhere inside it, Bliss curled around himself and charred like a cinder baby. He was surprised to feel regret.

Chi gave him the rest: Near as they could see, Stringer was down to four boys: Sheeny, Bronson, Turk, and one other. "Their horses would not have run far," she said. "Figure those men were out catching them before the fire got general."

"We'll see them soon," Cord guessed. "Right after the big burnout."

"Then we won't have long to wait," Oakley said.

He was right. Through the sooty haze shading the stars, the red glow of the fire line was almost to the north limits of the town.

It was an awesome and terrifying sight. The miles-long line of flames was about to close around the town like open arms. The basin had become Hell, and the empire of Mallory Bliss was his damnation.

The first flames reached the windmill, raced up the four legs, flared from the platform. The whirling blades fanned it and then were afire themselves as they continued to spin, throwing long streaks of flame into the night like some great carnival display on the Fourth of July.

Above the fire-front's great roar they heard the massive crackling rending sounds of wood giving way. The windmill was a great torch reaching above the smoke one hundred feet into the sky, teetering and twisting. It toppled majestically, almost elegantly. But that was the end of the elegant part.

The holding tank burst, sluicing water out with a huge

steaming hiss, though hardly slowing the fire's progress; it was like shooting at a bison with a .22. Buildings flared one after another, in twin lines running down either side of the main street. Last year's hay in the livery fed the conflagration there, and the building's roof collapsed. Across the street, the granite bank building seemed to be afire as well; at least wooden trim and the doors were burning. Then a window exploded, and another, and fire sluiced inside them.

"*Madre dios*," Chi breathed.

"No shit," Cord said. What a stick-stupid way to die. You could not face down or grapple with an enemy like this. Fire could sweep you away, as it had Bliss and all his life's ambition.

The two-story Enterprise House was engulfed now. Windows burst; the balcony splintered, sagged, and then fell to the street amid pluming sparks. The schoolhouse was burning as well, and fire licked over the granite walls of the adjacent library.

"The hell," Carlisle said sadly.

The roof of the Enterprise House buckled and fell into the gutted interior, and then the watching was over and the fire was on them. A great roaring wall of flame reared up before the ditch, flames fifteen feet high, pawing in air angrily as if momentarily nonplussed at the barrier formed by the brimming water sizzling at its rim, searching for some path across as to either side of the little house lot the arms of fire raced on to the south.

They were surrounded then. Cord spun around and saw flame everywhere. He could not find breath in the hot air, and sweat burned at his eyes. The fire was a great roaring hammer. *Chi*, he thought suddenly, and his panic washed away in concern for her. He could not see her through the smoke, but then he heard her call his name and staggered in that direction.

Fire lit the way ahead. Chi called, "Cord!" once more, and he saw her, ran to hold her.

But as he reached her, she thrust a bucket into his arms, and he realized that the side of Fiona Cobb's house was veneered with a thin sheet of flame. He stumbled to the ditch, moving toward the fire wall and fighting instinct. Carlisle was there already, dipping his bucket. He ran back past Cord, water slopping. Cord filled his own bucket, followed, flung the water against the house's siding. Fiona Cobb was slapping at the flame with a burlap sack, dropping to her knees in the muddy water to resoak it, beating angrily against the flame as if personally affronted. Off to the front of the house, the horses nickered out high terrorized whinnies.

Cord went back for more water. Out back the privy was lost, covered with fire. Chi was beside him, grabbing the full bucket, handing him an empty. "It's going to be all right," she shouted in his ear. He did not have the wherewithal to consider to what she referred. He dipped more water, dimly aware that the fire by the ditch was diminishing.

By the time he got back to the house, water splashing over his pant leg, it was over, quickly as it had come.

The fire wall was fifty feet past and screaming off to torment the southern half of the basin. Cord flung water against the house and steam billowed up, but the fire there was about extinguished as well. A little lick of it ran up the corner, and on the roof Oakley met it with a sack, beating it back. Most of the side of the house was scorched, but it was not going to burn down after all.

Cord dropped his bucket. It splashed in the ankle-deep water at his feet and turned over on its side, floated there.

"You okay?" Chi said quietly.

"Huh?" Cord stared at her as if she were a stranger. There was a smudge of soot across one of her cheeks. Cord wanted to wet his neckerchief and wipe it clean. Instead he said, "Yeah, terrific."

Oakley swung over the porch and plopped down into the water, looking soiled but whole. Carlisle licked at a livid red burn across the back of his hand, but he seemed all right as well. A thick strand of Fiona Cobb's dark hair had come loose and was plastered across the side of her face, and her shirt and jeans were smeared with mud. Cord realized he was mostly soaked himself, and shivered, though the hot wind blew unabated.

Out back of the house, the privy fell over, putting itself out with a sad hiss.

Chi took Cord's arm, and he almost jerked away. "Easy, *querido*," she murmured.

He looked at her. "Yeah." He shook his head. "Okay. All right."

The town that had called itself Enterprise was a smoldering ruin, shrouded by drifting smoke. Every building was leveled save the hulk of the brick bank building and the granite block that was the library; no telling how the latter had fared. Behind them the fire receded, its cry diminishing like a train already a good ways out of the depot. "Oakley?" Cord said, staring north across the town's rubble.

"I'm all right," Oakley said tightly.

"Let me look at that hand, Richard," Fiona Cobb said.

"It'll have to wait," Cord said.

Oakley came up beside him and Chi. "I am with you," he said, peering through the smoke.

"What is it?" Fiona Cobb said behind them.

"Look there," Chi said.

Starlight began to filter down to the basin's floor once more as the hot wind drove the smoke into their faces and on back, toward the fire flowering toward the mountains at the south rim. Still, acrid haze drifted everywhere. Fiona Cobb looked, holding Carlisle's hand tenderly.

At the far end of town, before the steaming ruins of the fallen windmill, Stringer and his four boys sat their horses, gazing on the end of things.

Stringer said something. Men dismounted, slapping their animals off to the side of the road. Cord blinked the sting from his eyes, fighting abiding weariness.

"Let's finish up." Chi was checking the chambers of her Colt. Her tone was matter-of-fact, just business. She looked up at Cord and gave him a little tight smile.

She was his strength, and he drew it in. She was waiting for him to set the play and give the orders. She could have done it, likely had some ideas, but she was waiting for him.

"I'll . . ." Carlisle began.

"You'll stay here," Cord interrupted. "Where are those two rifles of yours?" He turned and saw them on the porch. "You take one of them, Oakley."

Oakley tugged at his black leather gloves. "I can protect myself."

"Take the damned rifle," Cord said. He smiled to take the edge off. "Protect me, if you want."

Oakley considered. "Fair enough," he said, and went to the porch for the long gun.

Chi nodded, a tiny gesture of encouragement. Cord felt okay; he felt good. "Carlisle!"

Carlisle presented himself.

"You handle the other rifle," Cord said. "You and the

Doc stay here. We might need a safe place to fall back to."
Cord took Carlisle's measure. "You feel the horrors coming
on you, push them back. Take a drink—a little one—and
remember how you did fine with those thugs in your saloon."

"Worry about yourself, Cord." He was a little mad, and
that's how Cord wanted him.

Cord watched Fiona Cobb push hair out of her face.
"You keep your head down," he said. "We'll maybe want
some doctoring when this is done."

From up toward town, Stringer bellowed, "Cord!" The
word drifted like a curse on the hot filthy wind.

Cord gave Chi back her smile, then looked over to Oakley. "Like the lady said," Cord told him. "Let's finish up."

"They are dead," a man said.

"Fried like tough Texas steaks." It was the soft voice of
Sheeny.

"I want bodies!" Stringer hollered. "Find 'em, or make
'em."

Cord hunkered behind the high pile of charred lumber
that had been the Enterprise House. Wisps of smoke rose
from the still-warm wood. Among it, a few little flames
licked up around the blackened cast-iron stove, and the faint
smell of spilled whiskey perfumed the night air. Cord moved
up in a crouch along the collapsed back wall. Haze diffused
the starlight.

"If they are alive, they're likely holed up in that house,"
Sheeny said, somewhere across the street.

"With guns ready for us," Bronson said. "Waiting us
out."

"We'll storm it if we have to," Stringer snapped. "Ride
'em down like pigs. Now spread out and check around here.
That's first."

"Good way to get back-shot," someone grumbled.

"I will shoot you myself," Stringer barked, "you don't move out right this second."

Men's boots scuffed in the dirt in different directions.

Cord stayed where he was, his back to what was left of the wall, his gun ready, waiting, listening. After a minute or so he was rewarded by the small noise of someone edging toward the corner.

The man looked uneasy as he came around, gun up and dropping fast into a crouch, looking for ambush. Cord pressed into shadow. The man relaxed, looked around again more easily. Cord watched him grin as he got an idea. The man eased down on his haunches, gun still in hand but looking pleased with himself. His plan looked to involve staying out of trouble until the worst of it was over.

But on this night trouble was everywhere and time to get it rolling. Cord stepped out of the shadow and called softly, "Hey, there."

The man should have fired from his crouch, but he tried to stand, and Cord shot him in the chest. The dull crack of pistol fire cut above the last crackling sounds of burning, the echoes dying away as the man gagged and flopped on his back.

"Call out!" Stringer shouted from somewhere down the street toward the house.

No one answered. A single shot meant someone dead, no other way to read it. No one wanted to be next.

Cord eased down the alley between the saloon and the wreckage of the mercantile, got to where he could see across the street. It was spotted with puddles left from the flood of water from the windmill's burst tank.

Across the way, Chi stood in cover beside the hulk of the bank. She sensed him immediately, made a gesture.

Cord understood, nodded: she had one of them treed, even if the man didn't know it. . . .

Smoke drifted from the near front window of the bank. Chi edged up along the side of the building. Cord rotated the cylinder of his Colt back two positions, wrapping his hand around the frame to muffle the sound. At the corner of the building, Chi waved her gun.

Cord fired through the broken window, paused a beat, pulled the trigger again. The hammer fell on the empty cylinder. In case the sound were not loud enough, Cord swore, with feeling.

A rifle poked out the window, and its muzzle flashed fire. Cord was already down and behind cover.

The rifleman worked the lever, and Chi grabbed the barrel with her left hand, pulled hard. The gunman came half to his feet and Chi shot him in the face at point-blank range.

Chi pulled again, and Turk came out of the window and flopped over the sill, blood trilling in a little stream from his mouth and nose.

Cord covered her until Chi got Turk's rifle unpried from his dead fingers. She brought it up as Cord moved around the corner, eased along the front of the saloon's fallen balcony.

Down the street a gun went off. The blond man, Bronson, stood and dove headfirst from the roof of the library. He hit the stone steps with a sickening thud and slid down them into the street.

One wall of the schoolhouse stood precariously. Nick Oakley appeared from behind it, stared at Bronson's broken body, worked the lever of the rifle.

A gun went off behind Cord, the length of the street, and Oakley was hit. He stumbled backward, turned half-around, and went down on his side.

Cord dove for the street, hit, and rolled. A shot puffed into the dirt a yard from his head. He saw Sheeny in front of the smoking mercantile, reshouldering a rifle and aiming at him. Chi fired at Sheeny and missed by inches, and Cord fired on the echo of her shot. Wood splintered beside Sheeny's dark face. Sheeny dodged away, feeding another cartridge into his rifle's breech.

Cord struggled to his knees, steadied his left wrist on his bandaged right mitt this time, and shot Sheeny in the neck as he came up for another shot. Sheeny fell backward with his mouth open wide, a look of great surprise dissolving on his face.

Cord scrambled out of the open street. Four dead, the battle over except for Stringer. Cord's head suddenly pounded. His mouth tasted of ashes and bile, and his stomach was tossing. Cord squeezed his eyes shut for a long moment. The fight had rushed his hangover, and he was sick of blood and killing.

"Stringer!" he shouted.

Chi stood across the street before the bank, her rifle up, listening. Cord opened his eyes and peered down to where Oakley had been dropped.

Oakley was gone.

"Show yourself," Cord hollered.

"Look here," Stringer called.

The breeze swept the last of the haze aside, and there at the southern end of the street stood the big broad-shouldered bulk of Stringer, his back to Fiona Cobb's house. He held Nick Oakley up in front of him. A splotch of blood the size of a hand soaked the left shoulder of Oakley's shirt, but he was wide-eyed conscious. Stringer held the muzzle of his gun against Nick Oakley's head.

"Now let's have a look at you, you dirty son," Stringer

shouted. His nose was a swollen tuberous mass, and a trickle of blood ran down one side of his face from the cut on his forehead, opened somehow in the present fight. His voice edged toward madness.

"No!" Oakley hollered. The effort causing him to roll his head with pain. "Stay where you are. I'm done anyway."

No you are not, Cord thought, *not this time*. Cord looked across at Chi.

She frowned and shook her head. Everyone was out of ideas.

Cord rose. He stepped out into the street, holding his gun pointed at the ground. "Wait," Chi said softly. But there was no waiting. Stringer would shoot Oakley down, no question about it, and take his chances with them. He was that far gone, and the only chance was however many seconds cooperation bought them against the hope of some break, some miracle. . . . Cord moved down the street toward them.

"Drop it," Stringer ordered. "You, too, lady."

Cord took a few more steps. Stringer rammed the barrel of his gun into Oakley's temple. Oakley cried out. Behind Cord, Chi's rifle thudded to the ground.

"That's right," Stringer said. "Now you, Cord, right this second."

Cord dropped his gun to the mud of the street.

"Come closer, you bastard."

Cord advanced down the street, a step, another, another. Oakley came around and moaned, "You dumb farmer."

Cord kept coming.

"Right there is good." Stringer was liking this a lot.

Cord stopped five or six feet short of Stringer.

Stringer smiled crazily. He lowered the gun from Oakley's head, lined it on Cord's middle. Cord tensed, concentrated, tried to divine the moment of pressure of Stringer's finger on the trigger.

Behind Stringer, a gun exploded.

Stringer let go of Oakley, spun and crouched. Oakley fell away from him. Past Stringer, Cord caught a glimpse of Carlisle flopping flat to the ground as Stringer shot over his head.

Cord launched himself at Stringer.

Cord half fell on Stringer's back, rode him down to the muddy dirt. Cord grabbed for Stringer's gun wrist as Stringer bucked and twisted, rolled over. He was supine under Cord now, and Cord had Stringer's hand pinned.

But the man was maniacally strong. Stringer struggled to get his gun into play, bucking and kicking. His heavy-toed boot grazed Cord's shin, bringing a jolt of pain.

Cord cranked Stringer's wrist. Stringer bellowed and held on to the pistol. His face was inches from Cord's, blood all over one cheek, his eyes burning in their blackened sockets, his swollen lips bubbling spittle.

Cord butted Stringer under the chin. Stringer's teeth clacked together, but it was like butting a rock.

Yet it must have hurt Stringer as well, because as Cord lifted his head, pressing his body down on Stringer's, Cord saw the man's face screw up with pain. Cord gave one mighty wrench and snatched away Stringer's gun.

Stringer's eyes flashed. Cord jammed the gun into his side and pulled the trigger.

The big man stiffened and convulsed. Cord rode him like a twitching animal.

Stringer gave a mighty heave and threw Cord over on his back. Then Stringer was atop him, and both his hands were around Cord's throat.

Cord tried to cock the revolver, and his thumb slipped

off the scored surface of the hammer. He dug in, got the hammer pulled back, fired again. The report was muffled by Stringer's flesh.

Stringer screamed and squeezed harder. Cord felt the hard muscle of his windpipe collapsing. He fired again, worked the hammer, pulled the trigger a fourth time.

The gun clicked empty.

Cord let it go, grabbed at Stringer's fingers. It was like trying to open a bear trap. Stars burst before Cord's eyes, burst and went out.

Through the enshrouding blackness he saw Chi somewhere up above him, her hands high over her head and in them a rifle barrel. She swung, and the rifle's stock slammed against the back of Stringer's head, and the wood shattered, broke loose and cartwheeled away.

Stringer's entire body bowed and trembled terribly. He gasped, spraying a fine mist of blood in Cord's face. Then his limbs went limp, though his fingers stayed wrapped right around Cord's neck.

Cord clawed at them, choking under Stringer's suffocating dead weight. Chi's face was near to his, and then Carlisle beside her—the weight came off him.

Cord rolled away, came up against Oakley. Oakley groaned with pain, and Cord jerked away. "All I had was the rifle," Carlisle was explaining to someone. "I was afraid the bullet would have gone through and got Oakley. I hoped the noise would break up the action. . . ."

"Yeah," Cord said. "Good work."

Fiona Cobb was kneeling beside him. "See to Oakley," Cord said. Talking hurt. "I am okay."

But then he was not. His nostrils were choked with smells—smoke and blood and Stringer's awful stink. Cord pulled away, rolled over on his stomach, got to hands and knees. He wiped at his face and saw the gore on his palm. He could not have gotten to his feet had it meant life itself, and when he tried to crawl, he got only a few steps before he was sick.

Chapter Thirteen

CHI PAUSED WITH HER HAND ON THE DOOR-knob and regarded Cord. "You don't look too bad."

"Uh-huh," Cord agreed. "Hose me off and dress me in clean clothes, I'm a real prize."

"Yes, you are."

Cord flexed the fingers of his right hand. The swathing had come off, replaced with small patches of plaster. The blisters were scabbed over, and nothing hurt. "You ready?"

"For what?"

Cord shrugged. "Whatever you want."

Chi laughed gaily. "Let's take a ride. It's a nice day for a long ride."

"It will be," Cord agreed. "Soon as we get out of this place."

On the other side of the door, Nick Oakley called, "What's everybody so goddamned cheerful about?"

Chi opened the door. Oakley lay in the sickbed where Cord had awakened one long day ago. "This and that," Chi said to him. "Not being dead."

"You figure I am going to make it, eh?" Oakley said. His left shoulder was bandaged, and his arm was in a sling.

"We are all fine today," Chi assured him. She reached down and squeezed Oakley's hand. Cord didn't mind too much. She did look quite fine today—or maybe it was that all of life looked good, after the fight of only a half-dozen or so hours earlier.

"What about Bliss?" Oakley contradicted.

Chi sobered a bit. "Don't know. Carlisle will ride out there later on."

"If he made it," Oakley said, "he'd better keep away from me."

"Now, now," Cord chided. "He left something for you to remember him by." Cord dropped a thick packet of currency on the bed beside Oakley.

Oakley stared at the money.

"We got paid in advance," Chi told him. "You earned a share."

"That so?"

"Put it to good use," Chi said. "You aren't going to die, *chico*."

"Never?"

"Not from that shoulder. The *médica* took out the bullet and fixed you up." Chi hesitated. "You knew you weren't hurt bad."

Oakley shrugged. "That bastard was crazier than a drunken snake. I figured I was gone one way or the other—no point taking you with me."

Oakley studied Cord for a long moment. "I guess I would have been right, if you hadn't faced him down. Anyway, I noticed when you walked in that I'm not nursing any old grudges today."

Truth to tell, Cord liked hearing that. He'd never been too proud of the business in Denver. But apologizing was so damned hard, harder sometimes than facing guns. At least he'd thought so. . . .

"This is *adios*," Chi said to Oakley.

"See you again, maybe," Oakley said neutrally.

"You ever ride through the Bitter Root Valley," Chi said, "look around and see if we are there." She looked at Cord and laughed. "I will bake a sour-apple pie, and you old boys can sit in the porch rockers, smoking pipes and lying about your hellion days."

"Old boys?" Cord echoed. Chi laughed again and led him by the hand out of there. Oakley chuckled at their backs, but Cord could stand that as well.

They found Fiona Cobb and Carlisle out front, staring at what was left of the town. The ditch had been undammed and most of the water in the yard had settled into the scorched ground. The hot breeze was gone with the fire, and the day had dawned pleasant and cool. But the sun was rimmed in red, and without wind it would be days before the haze was all the way gone. Far off south in the mountains, the fire was still burning. The prairies were black in every direction.

Fiona Cobb's hand was cool and smooth when Cord shook it. "What are you two going to do?" Cord asked.

"Like you said," Carlisle laughed. "Pray for rain." Everyone was a little giddy with life today.

"We will stay," Fiona Cobb said. "Perhaps we will rebuild." She smiled. "On a smaller scale, I would say."

"We won't be starting from scratch." Carlisle shook his head. "You'll like this part, Cord. The fire sucked right into that bank, gutted it like a dead buck. But the library is whole, only a little scorching on the front door. Fire must have jumped right over it. We didn't lose a book."

Cord did like it. Hard to tell why; maybe he meant to become a serious book reader himself soon. Who could tell what would happen to a man with a settled life? "Time to go," he said, and climbed into the saddle.

"A moment," Chi said. She pointed. A rider was coming toward the wreckage of Enterprise. Cord peered through the haze and made out F. X. Connaught.

The little Irishman rode into the yard and looked from one of them to the other. "God's wrath is an awesome sight," he intoned.

"Yeah," Cord said. "We got to be going."

Connaught did not seem to hear. "We saw the fire, the men and I, as we neared the North Gap." He peered out across the wasteland. "I knew that Stringer had driven most of Mister Bliss's stock into the breaks, and could not abide what would befall them. I appealed to my men."

Connaught closed his eyes as if praying. "We rode back, rounded them up, and stampeded them through the gap. There are B-brand cattle scattered over a hundred square miles of country between the gap and the Missouri, but alive."

"Bliss?"

"May God preserve his soul."

No one else said anything. Cord cleared his throat significantly.

"Mister Connaught?" Fiona Cobb said gently.

Connaught opened his eyes and looked down at her.

"Will you take coffee?"

"Coffee." Connaught blinked. "Coffee would be fine." He swung down from the saddle, but then he looked up to Cord and Chi. "Go with God."

"Good idea," Cord said. He touched his finger to his hat brim and swung his horse away from there.

Out from the town the effect of the fire was not so devastating or troubling. The country was black and sere, but the grass would come back before the summer was out. This sort of burning was an old habit with nature. Land was a legacy no man could destroy, or perhaps truly own, Cord thought....

"Oh, my," Chi said.

Cord looked up from his reverie. To the west, maybe a hundred yards from the road, a couple of dozen blackened hummocks were scattered about the scorched earth. Cord felt a little jolt in his gut: the cows that had stampeded through town ahead of the fire storm, only to be caught here by the flames. Cord breathed through his mouth. Thank Christ there was no more wind....

Something moved: coming up from behind a little knoll, a man on horseback, a big man with long matted hair, sitting slump-shouldered on a soot-smeared pale horse.

It was Mallory Bliss, alone with his despair amid the excoriated corpses of his dream.

"Ought to tell him," Cord said slowly.

"He knows," Chi said gently. "Let him be."

A soft mournful sound drifted across the still air: Mallory Bliss was weeping.

"Yeah," Cord said, and headed the bay on south. On toward the Bitter Root Valley, and good news and greener pastures.

Afterword

ON JUNE 14, 1857, GRANVILLE STUART AND HIS older brother James, unsuccessful Sierra Nevada prospectors, left Yreka, California, for the home in West Liberty, Iowa, they had left five years earlier. There were nine other mounted men in the Stuart party and a half-dozen pack animals. Each rider had a muzzle-loading rifle, a Colt revolver, blankets, a change of underwear, and food for fifty or sixty days.

On July 27, when the party was near the present site of Malad City in southern Idaho, Granville became gravely ill. The men perceived he would recover slowly, if ever, and there was an amicable split up. The others rode on while James, once a physician's driver, remained to put what he had observed to work. Ill for seven weeks and certain as everyone else that he was a goner, Granville nevertheless recovered.

By then it was too late to proceed; before they could reach South Pass, snow would close out the route. The brothers could neither retrace their steps nor winter where they were, not without supplies and shelter.

Salt Lake City, a few days' ride south, was the most handy refuge. Unfortunately, during Stuart's convalescence, Utah Territory had become a war zone. When Brigham Young declared martial law and independence from the U.S., President Buchanan overreacted by sending in federal troops to crush the revolt. Young saw his bet and raised when his "Destroying Angels," for the nonce allied with indigenous Indians, massacred 120 gentile emigrants. In Utah, the Stuarts logically feared, they were odds on to be executed for spies.

During the forced layover, the Stuarts had become friends with a one-time mountain man named Jake Meeks. Meeks was now a road rancher, trading his grass-fat cows for Mormon Trail emigrants' foot-sore oxen, one for two. In winter Meeks grazed his stock in the clement valley of the Beaverhead River, two hundred miles north, and he invited the Stuarts to come along.

The historian seeking drama in true life could attach great significance to October 10, 1857, the date the Stuarts crossed the divide and looked down at Montana for the first time. Stuart does when sixty years later he describes his descent into the Beaverhead. In his recollection, the bunch grass turns thick as carpeting and the weather warm and bright, and the antelope run in packs of twenty.

But on that day, it did not occur to Granville Stuart that he and his brother would make their homes for the rest of their days in Montana or that he would become the single most influential figure in the development of the society and economics of the future state. In the autumn of 1857,

Stuart was concerned only with blizzards and crazed Mormons, and keeping his ass out of the road of both.

In the twinings of a peripatetic career, Granville Stuart sought his fortune as prospector, miner, mercantilist, writer, gunsmith, blacksmith, butcher, sawyer, horse trader, real estate speculator, banker, rancher, and diplomat. Paradoxically, perplexingly, in not one of these pursuits was he ever able to turn a real profit.

Stuart's peers consistently elected him to public office, suggesting he was neither incompetent nor lazy. Stuart was variously president of the Deer Lodge Town Committee; chair of the Deer Lodge County Commissioners; a trustee of school districts, Montana's first college, and the territorial prison; and a five-term member of the territorial legislature.

Within a few years of his arrival in Montana, Stuart attracted respect as a historian, librarian, bibliophile, conservationist, artist, and vigilante. In one year, 1871, a Stuart essay was published in the *New York Times*; he was appointed statistical correspondent to the Smithsonian Institution; and in answer to a query, he informed a no-doubt disappointed freak-show impressario named P. T. Barnum that Flathead Indians did not in fact have flat heads.

Yet as Paul C. Phillips, editor of Stuart's autobiography, writes, Stuart and his brother James

> broke the sod but others reaped the harvest. They gave to the world knowledge of the gold resources of Montana but they themselves panned but little of the precious metal. . . . They were the first merchants of the gold mining era but others garnered the profits. And finally when Granville Stuart embarked in a business that brought him wealth, conditions beyond his control overwhelmed him with financial ruin.

For one thing, Stuart was too generous to succeed in business. He habitually extended credit with reckless disregard for the customer's ability to repay, while his own creditors were less charitable.

For another, Stuart did seem to have more than his share of hard luck. As an example: in 1865, when Montana was seven months old, Stuart published the first book on the new territory, *Montana as It Is*, brought out by C. S. Westcott of New York. It contains a history of the gold strikes, topological descriptions, a vocabulary of Snake and the Chinook patois, ethnological comments on the Indians of Montana, travel routes, and anecdotes. Of the 1,500 copies printed, 1,100 were destroyed within weeks in a warehouse fire back east. Of the remainder, 100 were sent to Stuart on a bull wagon and were seriously water damaged during the trip. Stuart claimed the remaining 300 were stolen by acting territorial governor James Tufts and sold for his profit.

A third factor in Stuart's lifelong run of debt and disappointment was his short attention span. Paul Robert Treece, Stuart's biographer, notes that

> while fate seems to have dealt perversely with Stuart, his inability to concentrate long on any one particular vocation is the major explanation why Stuart, despite his leadership qualities, never achieved a position of wealth similar to that of many of his more single-minded acquaintances.

Stuart freely admitted that he liked to daydream. Noting one trip to prospect Gold Creek, Stuart confided to his diary that instead of panning, he "read Byron and indulged in many reveries." On another, lulled by the babble of the presumably auriferous creek, he fell asleep under a tree.

With some self-deprecation, Stuart himself laid the blame on a striking image from his school days.

> For text books we had Webster's spelling book, with that discouraging frontispiece, a picture of a very lightly clad young man weakening when half way up a high mountain with a little cupola on top of it and on its front gable the word "Fame," in large letters, and a rough looking female ordering him to climb or bust. I attribute my failure to achieve greatness to that picture. The constant contemplation of it so impressed the difficulty of being famous (in that costume) upon my youthful mind that hope died within me.

Webster's influence complemented that of Stuart's father, who moved his family five times in Stuart's first nine years, always westward. Robert Stuart left by himself for the California goldfields in 1849, and returned only long enough to fetch his two boys with him on the second trip—not only because he needed mine hands, but also from a desire to share the adventure. Granville and James said good-bye to their father a few weeks after arriving in California and did not see him again before his death in 1861.

Of course, the Stuarts never found more than day wages in their gold pans. They prospered more as laborers and market hunters and had no plans beyond a brief family visit when they left California in 1857. As Treece says, "The sum of Granville Stuart's California experience was to render him . . . unfit for regular employment for decades." In hindsight it is clear that Granville's illness and the Mormon troubles that sent him north to Montana were a rare stroke of good luck. He would not have been happy in Iowa anyway.

*   *   *

The patriarch of the Beaverhead was Richard Grant, a querulous old Hudson's Bay Company trapper who demanded the title "Captain." Grant had wintered a few head of shorthorns in the valley as early as 1850 and now lived in the only proper home, a three-room log cabin. The remainder of the five dozen or so Europeans present lived in elk-hide tepees; nearly all were Captain Grant's relatives or employees. The other locals included small groups of Bannock, Snake, Nez Perce, and Flathead who had set up their lodges in the vicinity when the Stuarts came into the country in the fall of 1857.

The winter was mild, and during its course James and Granville acquired twenty horses in trade with the Indians. On March 28, 1858, they started for Fort Bridger, in the southwestern corner of Wyoming, but a late-season blizzard drove them back. In their dilatory way, the Stuarts drifted over to the Deer Lodge Valley, where they happened to hear rumors of gold traces discovered some time earlier by a French Canadian trader named François Findlay and known as Benetsee. The Stuarts were no more wedded to the notion of Fort Bridger than they had been to the notion of Iowa, and headed instead for Benetsee Creek (now Gold Creek), above the Clark Fork sixty miles east of Missoula.

A half century later, Granville Stuart lobbied the Montana Legislature to grant him an annuity in recognition of his first discovery of gold in the state. In his petition, Stuart wrote that his test hole was "the first prospecting for gold done in what is now Montana and . . . the first real discovery of gold within the state."

Stuart's claim was specious, and he knew it. At the time of his own prospect, Stuart freely acknowledged Benetsee's find in 1852 and admitted that he was tipped off to the spot by other men who had found color there, probably including an associate of Captain Grant, Robert Hereford, who panned the creek in 1856. Various historians have suggested at least a dozen others as the first discoverer of Montana gold.

Stuart neither improved on Benetsee's six-year-old prospect nor started a rush. In fact, Stuart never washed more than ten cents to the pan on Gold Creek, did not post a claim, and did not return for two years, although during that time he lived nearby. His discovery was perfectly ordinary; you can get color in a pan of Gold Creek gravel today, but not enough to come out any better than Stuart did in the same spot 130 years earlier.

During the next few years the Stuarts traded stock and furs between southwestern Montana and northern Utah, with modest success. By 1861 they owned over eighty beeves and some horses and were genuine settlers. They lived in a cabin, kept chickens and milk cows, and bought flour, sugar, and salt at Frank Woody's mercantile sixty miles down the Clark Fork, on the Mullan Road near the present site of Missoula. The country was opening up; the first Missouri River steamboat had reached Fort Benton the previous spring, and from there teamsters hauled freight down the Mullan Road all the way to Fort Walla Walla in Washington.

But what opened the country for all time was gold, the same gold that had eluded the Stuarts. In late 1861 two of their neighbors finally found Benetsee's fabled prospect. But when the rush to Gold Creek did not amount to much, the newcomers ranged further afield, and in the gulch country between the Madison and Ruby rivers found paying placers. Between 1862 and 1865, boomtowns sprang up at Bannack, Virginia City, Nevada City, and Alder Gulch.

The Stuarts prospected most of these places, with their usual luck. So they turned to boomtown business, profiting moderately through trading, gunsmithing, butchering beef, market hunting, and speculating in real estate. As old Montana hands, both became community leaders. In 1862 James was elected first sheriff of Missoula County, which at the time comprised most of Montana west of the divide. In 1865, Granville was commissioned a lieutenant-colonel in the territorial militia.

The Montana fields eventually produced about ten million dollars of gold; in comparison, nearly one billion dollars, one hundred times as much, came out of the Sierra Nevada deposits in California. But gold in Montana was the first explosion in a chain reaction.

In 1866 a Texas cattleman named Nelson Story drove six hundred sinewy longhorns from Dallas to Virginia City, fifteen hundred miles in six months. His was the longest and most famous of many drives that within fifteen years brought hundreds of thousands of cows to the open ranges of central and eastern Montana, where only buffalo and deer had grazed before. When the natives reacted to this imperialism with hostility, the government established a network of army forts to protect the invaders. The soldiers in turn supplied a new market for trade goods. The Missouri and Yellowstone rivers were further developed as shipping routes, and military and private surveyors crisscrossed the territory with roads.

During this period, the Stuarts did a little prospecting, pursued all their old trades, added part ownership of a quartz smelter and a lumber mill to their portfolio of bad investments, and shared with each other their daydreams. Granville wanted to be a travel writer, and both brothers had a schoolboylike fondness for Latin America. At one point, James tried to persuade their influential friend Samuel T.

Hauser, who would later be governor, to secure for him the appointment as U.S. consul to Honduras.

While Granville Stuart's financial fortunes changed little during these two decades of Montana's greatest growth and development, his personal fortunes took two debilitating blows. The first occurred on April 15, 1862, when he married a twelve-year-old full-blooded Shoshone named Awbonnie Tookanka. Stuart was twenty-seven.

At least through the 1860s, male settlers vastly outnumbered female, and most took Indian or mixed-blood women as common-law wives. These marriages were casually made and casually dissolved. Granville's previous wife had run off ten days before he took Awbonnie, and James had several wives and two children over the years. But when civilization, and civilized women, came into the country, the notion of the squaw man took on currency. Wives of native blood were viewed as whores or savages.

Most men solved the problem by abandoning or banishing their wives and children. Granville Stuart remained married to Awbonnie for twenty-six years, until her death in 1888 liberated him from the one turn of fate in his life he rued most, the step he blamed for his greatest failures.

In his autobiography, Stuart includes the diary entry noting the marriage and then never mentions Awbonnie again. But in other writings, his conflict, and the terrible burden that he considered his marriage to be, is clearly limned. In early 1866, for example, in a letter to James reporting his first visit home in fourteen years, Granville writes that their mother reacted to the news of their marriages as if both were "a little more wicked than the inhabitants of Sodom & Gomorrah." Stuart describes the attractive single women in their east Iowa hometown and continues, "If I wasn't quite *so much married* already, I think I would have to succumb to the pressure . . . to drown my outfit. . . ."

The next year the Stuarts' younger brother, Sam, and his family moved to Montana. Sam's wife, Amanda, demonstrated her disdain for her sisters-in-law by dressing in blankets and aping them. Soon after, the Sam Stuarts returned to Iowa.

In April of 1873, while on his way back from a visit home during which his life-style was criticized anew, Granville met four men on the train to Cheyenne. One claimed to have observed a massive but ill-publicized gold strike in French Guiana. This news played to Granville's two favorite fantasies: striking it rich and traveling to South America. In a letter to James, he proposed chucking it all:

> It will give me a chance to reconstruct my social basis & close out my present family arrangements for I shudder with horror when I contemplate getting old in my present fix, or ever to get poor would be awful. . . . my repugnance to my present mode of life increases daily. . . . just think of having to go anywhere with such an outfit as mine. On the [train] cars for instance & then to settle in a strange place & live in defiance of public opinion as we have always done . . . with my present outfit I can never go anywhere. . . . I could never marry any respectable high toned woman after [my] conduct.

A photographic portrait reveals Awbonnie to be a compact clean-featured woman with dark skin and straight black hair. She bore eleven children with Granville Stuart and raised James's two sons, Robert and Richard, with such devotion that for years they thought themselves her natural issue. Awbonnie Tookanka Stuart died of a fever at the age of thirty-eight, twenty days after the birth of her last child.

Granville Stuart was fervently irreligious, so his stoic devotion must be attributed to a sense of ethics and responsibility, and a lifelong belief that one lay in the bed one made. It is also possible he loved his wife. By all accounts, Stuart never ill-treated her or his mixed-blood children, or publicly demonstrated his ambivalent feelings. On the contrary, he was solicitous of the family's health and welfare as long as Awbonnie lived. As their children grew, he assured they were educated, hiring teachers and opening the school to his neighbors' offspring. In later years several of Stuart's children remembered their father's reading to them aloud from volumes in his three-thousand book library.

The second blow to Granville Stuart's grand vision was James's unexpected death of liver disease on September 30, 1873. James was forty-two.

The brothers had spent their entire lives together. All their ventures were jointly pursued, and Stuart believed the unit they formed was greater than its parts. "We were much nearer and dearer to each other than brothers usually are," Stuart wrote his mother after James's death. "We . . . passed through many perils unscathed and our lives were so closely knit together that the separation is dreadful beyond all description to me. I feel like my life was shipwrecked shattered, & that all our toiling & struggling had been in vain since he is taken from us."

As Treece notes, "Gone were the dreams of discovering that elusive eldorado, establishing a successful business or industry, authoring and illustrating travel books, or achieving great political or financial success because all of them had included James." For Stuart, James's death left "a gap in my life that will never close."

I felt like forever abandoning these familiar scenes where everything reminds me of the pleasant hours I have spent among them with poor James, and that all our many plans of what we would do in coming years are now wrecked and sunk in the sea of death. The enjoyment that either of us took in anything was always in proportion to the pleasure it gave the other.

Stuart, who was generally too busy for illness, now complained of malaise and ordered "heart pills" by mail. His illness was likely psychosomatic, but the destitution that caused it was real enough. Stuart would recover his health, but he would never fully recover his zest.

In 1879 Stuart partnered up with his old friend Sam Hauser and two other investors in a cattle-raising enterprise capitalized at $150,000. Stuart kicked in $20,000, which he borrowed from Hauser's bank. He was appointed ranch manager, and he journeyed to Oregon, Deer Lodge, and Sun River Valley to buy stock. By the fall of 1880, Stuart had driven five thousand head of cattle and sixty horses into the great grassy range of the Judith Basin and erected his ranch house near some year-round cold springs on Ford's Creek.

Stuart summed up his prospects in an article for the Deer Lodge newspaper. "In five or six years the ranges will begin to exhaust," he wrote. "In the meantime, with ordinary good luck, there is 'big money' in the business."

Stuart's first prediction was extraordinarily prescient. As to his second, he was still unaware that "ordinary good luck" was a commodity with which he was not blessed. Although by 1883 Stuart was running 12,000 fat shorthorns and turning a steady profit, his reputation and fortune would suffer due to two incidents, one an unfortunate act of man, the other an act of nature.

The rustler problem in central Montana and Granville Stuart's activities as leader of the vigilante group that came to be known as Stuart's Stranglers is discussed in our afterword to the second book in the Cord series, *The Nevada War*. However, Treece's research turns up several less savory aspects of the adventure, in which at least seventeen men were executed.

One member of the Stranglers had a criminal record and was later convicted of killing a sheepman in a drunken rage. This did not inflame contemporary opinion in some corners as much as the killing of Dixie Burr, Stuart's own nephew, or the hanging of Billy Downes. Downes had friends who considered him an honest man, and although the 26 horses the Stranglers found at his cabin could have been stolen, Downes's Indian wife claimed he had obtained them in a legitimate trade, unaware of their origin. Notwithstanding significant local objection to the vigilantes and some community resentment directed at Stuart, the cattlemen were pleased. The next year the Montana Stock Growers Association elected Stuart president.

Not long after, Stuart's prediction about the range's longevity came tragically true. A drought in the summer of 1886 was followed by the most vicious winter in memory. Stuart's Pioneer Cattle Company lost at least two-thirds of its 40,000 head. The next spring, after surveying the rotting carcasses piled in the coulees, Stuart wrote, "I never wanted to own again an animal I could not feed and shelter." He need not have worried. With the massive winterkill, the ranch failed and Stuart could not meet his loan payments. He was allowed to keep a single token share of Pioneer

Cattle Company stock; aside from it, he was bankrupt once again.

On January 8, 1890, a little more than a year after Awbonnie's death, Stuart married Allis Belle Brown Fairfield, twenty-six, a one-time teacher at Stuart's ranch schoolroom. During the courtship she was living with her parents in the Bitter Root Valley at Grantsdale, the town founded by Captain Richard Grant, Stuart's first friend in Montana. The marriage had the peculiar and regrettable result of succeeding where nearly thirty years of social opprobrium had failed: It utterly sundered Granville Stuart's family.

The Brown family had come to Philipsburg, Montana, from western Iowa in 1879. Some time later, Allis Belle returned east to attend the Northern Indiana Normal College at Valparaiso and may also have been at Vassar. After college she taught in Johnson County, Wyoming, where she was briefly married to a man named Fairfield.

The Stuart children disliked Allis Belle with a vehemence only partially explained by the discoverable facts. Their accusations of bigotry were probably true; Allis Belle surely shared the prevalent prejudice toward children of mixed blood. How overtly she demonstrated her bigotry and how Stuart reacted are conjectural, because the children's other accusations are so clearly biased that their credibility is undermined.

Mary Stuart, eighteen, and herself newly married to Teddy Blue Abbott, one of her father's cowhands, was convinced Allis Belle was a harlot and may have meant the accusation literally. According to Mary, during Allis Belle's one-term tenure as schoolteacher, she had carried on an open affair with Will Burnett, Stuart's foreman. Mary believed that the Wyoming marriage to Fairfield was a sham as well. In a letter to Teddy Blue before their marriage, Mary concluded, "Well Ted she is very pretty but did you ever see one that wasn't?"

All of this smacks of girlish gossip flavored with a dash of Electra complex, except that the older and more temperate Teddy Blue is even more vituperative in his opinion of Allis Belle. Teddy Blue, like his father-in-law a diarist and eventual autobiographer, was a well-liked open-minded man who would remain married to Mary until his death forty-nine years later. Yet in diary entries postdating Stuart's marriage, Abbot writes, "I pity Granville Stuart. . . . I feel ashamed of him tonight. . . . It makes me Hot to think [he] would ever marry such a thing." In other entries, Abbott calls Allis Belle Stuart a "hag," "Bitch," and "Whore."

At the beginning of 1890, six of Stuart's children lived at home, but within a few months, tension overwhelmed the household. On March 26 James's son, Richard, lit out for Canada. The next day Elizabeth Stuart, sixteen, left or was expelled by Allis Belle and went to live with her older sister, Mary, and her husband, Teddy Blue. Soon afterward, the remaining four children were placed in the Saint Ignatius Catholic Mission School on the Flathead Reservation north of Missoula. They were Sam, thirteen; Edward, nine; Harry, five; and Irene, two. Granville Stuart, conscientious though tortured husband and father for twenty-six years, had abandoned his family absolutely.

Edward immediately ran away from the church school to live with Mary and Teddy Blue. Sam remained for about a year before returning to central Montana and hiring on as a hand, where he achieved some fame for his cowboying skills and was subsequently featured in a *Life* magazine article. Harry was adopted by a Flathead named John B. Findlay, possibly a descendant of François "Benetsee" Findlay, whose gold prospects Stuart explored thirty-two years earlier. Harry died in 1906 at the age of twenty and was buried on the reservation.

Irene's fate is obscured by contradictory hearsay and the loss of mission records in two fires in the early part of this century. One tale has her dying as a child; in this version the Sisters consult Allis Belle Stuart for instructions, and the curt reply is "Bury her." In another, Irene becomes Sister Marie and visits Rome.

What is uncontradicted is that Stuart's contact with his children was minimal to nonexistent from here on. Several years after the marriage, Stuart's oldest son, Tom, was committed by a judge, on the advice of two doctors, to the state insane asylum at Warm Springs. Stuart was not involved in the decision and never mentioned the episode.

To complete Stuart's personal purgatory, he was now reduced to the one job he had hated and feared all his life, the job his father had fled for the goldfields forty years earlier. Stuart became a dirt farmer, living by the owners' forbearance on the ranch he had once managed and part owned, a fifty-six-year-old man in coveralls and straw hat hoeing a truck garden.

In March 1891, Stuart, a lifelong Democrat, was emancipated by Montana's first Democratic governor, Joseph K. Toole, who appointed Stuart state land agent. Stuart used this reprieve to petition every influential friend he could think of, soliciting a position worthy of his impressive background. It was three years before Stuart hit pay dirt, incidentally fulfilling his lifelong dream of visiting South America. On March 1, 1894, President Grover Cleveland appointed Stuart to the post of U.S. envoy extraordinary and minister plenipotentiary to Paraguay and Uruguay, at an annual salary of $7,500.

Stuart's instinctive social grace, patience, and intelligence overcame any handicap from spending his life outside the States, and historians give him good marks as a diplomat. Allis Belle Stuart loved being an ambassador's wife, but Stuart was less taken with the foofaraw. "The social duties of a Minister are just awful," Stuart wrote to a Montana friend, "and as you well imagine that sort of thing comes about as natural to me as climbing a tree does to a fish."

But neither age nor the exotic venue improved Stuart's fiscal prudence. He continued his optimistic search for one great strike-it-rich scheme with undimmed enthusiasm.

His predecessor, a bachelor, lived at a private club, and the legation in Montevideo was a ramshackle, ill-furnished place. Stuart rented new quarters, remodeling and furnishing at his own expense. Attaché to Paraguay as well, he traveled frequently, and always he kept his eye open to opportunity.

Observing the stock-growing industry on the broad plains drained by the Rio de la Plata, Stuart became convinced that he could do it better and make a fortune by the way. Land, water, and wages were dirt-cheap; there were neither rustlers, disease, nor predators; and the weather was mild year-round. To his old patron Sam Hauser, Stuart wrote:

> I understand the business thoroughly and can improve upon some of their methods of raising cattle. . . . I want to buy from 80 to 100 square miles . . . with 10,000 cattle to begin with. . . . Now I want you to assist me in borrowing this money in New York. You can testify to my honesty & ability and my present position is evidence of my standing. . . . Now Sam this is no rose colored impracticable dream of mine. . . .

Stuart had that part dead wrong. For one thing, another international depression had driven the economy to a nadir; Hauser's First National Bank of Helena had gone belly-up in the summer of 1896. For another, Stuart's personal financial condition was, as always, precarious. He owned virtually no capital assets, and for at least the prior thirty years had never lived a debt-free day. He was a credit risk no prudent lender would assume.

Not long after, the election of President William McKinley put Stuart out of work. In the few months before he was replaced by a Republican newspaper editor from Wisconsin, Stuart traveled extensively in South America and bought trunk loads of books. He returned to Montana in June 1898 about as broke as when he left.

The Stuarts settled in Butte, where they managed a boardinghouse called the Dorothy. Stuart begged Hauser for loans, pursued old fiscal wrongs in court without notable success, and in 1905 became the head librarian of the Butte Public Library. Allis Belle was variously a shop clerk and a hairdresser. Stuart retired from the library in 1914 and devoted himself to his writings, completing most of his autobiography before his death, of heart disease, on October 2, 1918, at the age of eighty-four. Despite his explicit instructions to the contrary, he was given a church funeral.

Besides the autobiography, Stuart at his death had been writing a multivolume illustrated Montana history that stood at 314,000 words. Although Mrs. Stuart solicited influential patrons, among them George Bird Grinnell, the history was essentially unpublishable, and after a number of rejections, she gave up.

After her husband's death, Allis Belle Stuart lived in various communities in Montana, Idaho, and Colorado, eventually settling in the Bitter Root Valley in 1930. She worked as a Spanish translator for the federal government, a researcher for the WPA Writers' Project, and a ranch cook. After suffering two strokes, she was forced to accept public welfare assistance, which was supplemented through the kindness of neighbors and friends. She was living in the home of Hamilton postmaster C. A. "Pete" Smithey when she died of a cerebral hemorrhage on March 31, 1947. There are dozens of people living in the Bitter Root today who knew Allis Belle Stuart well and recall her with affection.

In Montana, there is a popular image of Stuart in his last years: a kindly old gent, surrounded by the books he loved all his life and fondly, perhaps dotishly, recalling pioneer days on the great open plains, while autos chug by on Butte's busy streets and the copper smelters spew great industrious billows of sooty smoke into the Big Sky.

But the evidence, augmented by the recollections of those who were there, limn a different, more complex man. Granville Stuart had seen some things and been some places and had nothing for it but the memories he was trying frantically to document at his death. He'd sat at many a table, but by the time the gravy boat got to him it was invariably empty.

Because he was unaware of his weaknesses, Stuart believed life had dealt him an endless series of Yarboroughs and cursed his fate. He did not die a serene bibliophile; he died a bitter, cynical, frustrated old man who had been stripped of all his gods. It was the way Granville Stuart was and, we suspect, the way he would prefer to be remembered.

Granville Stuart's autobiography, published in 1925 as *Forty Years on the Frontier as seen in the Journals and Reminiscences of Granville Stuart, Gold-Miner, Trader,*

Merchant, Rancher and Politician, remains in print in two volumes retitled *Prospecting for Gold; From Dogtown to Virginia City, 1852–1864*; and *Pioneering in Montana; The Making of a State, 1864–1887*. Among his protean skills, Stuart was an artist of some talent; a noteworthy selection of his drawings was published in 1963, nearly a century after they were made, as *Diary & Sketchbook of a Journey to "America" in 1866, & Return Trip up the Missouri River to Fort Benton*.

The most exhaustive Stuart biography is *Mr. Montana: The Life of Granville Stuart, 1834–1918*, an unpublished Ph.D. dissertation by Paul Robert Treece, presented in 1974 at Ohio State University. An accessible contemporary account of aspects of Stuart's cattleman days, including the story of Stuart's Stranglers, is *We Pointed Them North: Recollections of a Cowpuncher*, by E. C. Abbott ("Teddy Blue") and Helena Huntington Smith. Chapter 2 of *The Ranchers* volume in the Time-Life Old West series places Stuart's endeavors against the background of the rise and first fall of stock raising in Montana. It reproduces photographs of James and Granville Stuart and both of Granville's wives, as well as several of Stuart's sketches. The text is by Ogden Tanner.

William Kittredge
Steven M. Krauzer
Missoula, Montana
Autumn, 1985

About the Author

Owen Rountree is the pseudonym of Steven M. Krauzer and William Kittredge, who live in Missoula, Montana. Kittredge, Professor of English at the University of Montana, has published two collections of short stories, most recently *We Are Not In This Together*, edited by Raymond Carver (Graywolf Press, Port Townsend, Washington). As Adam Lassiter, Krauzer is the author of the *Dennison's War* series of action thrillers. Two of his screenplays have been filmed, and he is currently working on a television miniseries.

GREAT TALES
from the
OLD WEST

OWEN ROUNTREE